Critics rave about Simon Brett and his Charles Paris mysteries!

"Quite simply the best in the business!"
—*Kirkus Reviews*

"Brett knows the British stage inside out, and backgrounds are unusually authentic."
—Newgate Callendar,
The New York Times Book Review

"Paris is probably current crime fiction's most complex and developed series character and . . . Simon Brett is the best serial mystery writer now setting pen to paper."
—*Sun-Times* (Chicago)

"Simon Brett, the Laurence Olivier of the theatrical mystery, writes thrillers that play wonderfully: the dialogue is witty and natural, the characterization engagingly complex, and the plots most cunningly constructed."
—*Booklist*

AN AMATEUR CORPSE

Simon Brett

A DELL BOOK

Published by
Dell Publishing Co., Inc.
1 Dag Hammarskjold Plaza
New York, New York 10017

Dell ® TM 681510, Dell Publishing Co., Inc.

ISBN: 0-440-10185-9

Reprinted by arrangement with Charles Scribner's Sons
Printed in the United States of America
May 1986

10 9 8 7 6 5 4 3 2 1

WFH

Dedicated to
SOPHIE

One...

THE CAST PARTY for the Breckton Backstagers' production of *The Seagull* was held, like all their cast parties, in the rehearsal room. Drinks were served in the bar (known to the members as the Back Room) and were paid for by a collection made during the run by the Assistant Stage Manager. The choice, displayed on the bar, was cheap Spanish red in two-litre bottles or cheap Spanish white in two-litre bottles.

Charles Paris was the first to arrive in the Back Room after the curtain fell on the Saturday night. His friend Hugo Mecken had stopped off in the Gents on the way from the theatre. The cast were still creaming off their make-up and slipping out of costumes and most of their hangers-on were hanging on in the dressing rooms, spraying out wild congratulations and faint praise. Hugo, Charles noticed without surprise, had not gone backstage to congratulate his wife Charlotte on her performance as Nina.

Charles was conscious of his interloper status. So,

judging from his sour expression, was the thin man in a cravat who stood behind the bar. Charles tried. "A glass of red, please."

"Are you a member?"

It was a perfect example of what Charles remembered being taught about in Latin school—a question expecting the answer no. It got it.

"Then I'm afraid I can't give you a drink."

"My name is Charles Paris. I was invited down here this evening to see the show because I'm leading the Critics' Circle discussion on Tuesday."

"Ah. Well, in that case, a member will be able to get you a drink."

"But I can't get one for myself?"

"Not unless you are a member."

Charles was beginning to get angry. "And how much would it cost me to become a bloody member?"

"Two pounds a year Social Membership or five pounds Acting Membership. Though for that, of course, you have to pass an audition."

With difficulty Charles didn't say what he thought of the idea of himself, as a professional actor, having to audition for a tin-pot suburban amateur dramatic society. He channelled his annoyance into slamming two pounds down on the counter. "Right, there you are. I'm a Social Member. Now give me a drink."

"I'm afraid your application has to be endorsed by a member."

Hugo appeared slap on cue from the Gents. "Right, here's my endorsing member—Hugo Mecken. I'm Charles Paris, there's my two pounds, now give me a drink."

"What's the trouble, Charles?" asked Hugo.

"I'm joining the bloody society, so that I have a licence to breathe in this place."

"Oh, you don't need to—"

"I've joined. Red wine, please."

"And for me too, Reggie."

Sour Reggie paused for a second, searching for another rule that was being contravened. Failing to find one, he ungraciously half-filled two wine-glasses.

They drank. Charles contemplated Hugo. Olive-colored skin, his head a bald dome fringed with black hair, dark eyes darting about uneasily. The lips, heavy with indulgence in the good things of life, turned down, registering that the Backstagers' Spanish plonk wasn't among them.

Charles was conscious of the silence. He often had difficulty in thinking of what to say to Hugo. It had always been the same, even when they first met at Oxford back in 1947. They had been friends, but conversation had never flowed easily.

And when they had remet a couple of months previously it had been exactly the same. A great warmth, affection for each other, but not a lot to say. A good working-relationship, socially no overt strain. Just a slight tension within Charles from a sense of Hugo's dependence on him. Hugo was almost too hospitable, inviting Charles down to Breckton all the time, pressing a spare house key on him, telling him to use the place as his own.

But the re-established contact had been a godsend at least from the financial point of view. Hugo seemed likely to put a lot of work his way after what had been a very lean year, even by the modest standards of Charles Paris's theatrical career.

Hugo Mecken was the Creative Director of Mills Brown Mazzini, a small but thriving advertising agency in Paddington, and he had introduced Charles to the lucrative world of commercial voice-over work. It was a strange world to Charles, one that he was still trying to come to terms with, to fit into his picture of what being an actor meant.

The pause had gone on too long for comfort. "Charlotte's very good," Charles volunteered.

"Should be. Professionally trained." The shortness of Hugo's response confirmed his suspicion that all was not well with the marriage.

"I feel like getting obscenely pissed," Hugo continued suddenly, and drained his glass.

It was a familiar cry. The word "pissed" was of the seventies but the intention was one which Charles had often heard from Hugo thirty years before at Oxford. Sometimes it had been a danger signal. A sudden lurch of mood, a lot to drink and then bizarre midnight exploits, wild destruction of college windows or other fierce extravagances until the passion subsided into somnolence and, later, self-abasing recrimination.

While Hugo outstared sour Reggie into refilling their glasses Charles reviewed his friend's marital history. First wife, Alice, married straight out of Oxford. Rather swish do in Worcester College Chapel at which Charles had been present. Two children soon after, all set on conventional course.

Then, over twenty years later, news from a mutual friend, Gerald Venables, that Hugo had contacted him in his professional capacity as a solicitor and wanted a divorce. He had upped and left Alice with two teenagers, and moved in with some twenty-two-year-old actress with whom he'd done a commercial.

A couple of years later, a scribbled note on Snoopy paper (strong contrast to the heavy die-stamped invitation to Worcester Chapel) asked Charles to a post-registry office piss-up in an expensive Soho trattoria.

Through hazes of alcohol, Charles could recall that riotous meal. Hugo and Charlotte dressed in identical oyster-grey velvet suits, a lot of advertising people, a lot of showbiz. A truly glittering occasion. Charlotte so young, so unbelievably beautiful, her complexion glowing and red hair sparkling in the colored lights of the restaurant. And Hugo boisterous as a schoolboy, his bald dome gleaming, his face alive with the knowledge that every man in the room envied him.

Then it had all seemed possible. That one could start again. It even convinced Charles how right he had been to leave his own wife Frances. Somewhere, round some corner, there was a perfect young girl waiting for him, someone who could make it all happen again.

Mostly it had been the drink thinking for him. But there had been more than that. Hugo, in a good mood, was a fierce romantic and he could infect others with his enthusiasm. He could make everyone believe that the world was perfectible, that it was only a matter of time before paradise was re-established on earth.

Charles remembered acting in a play which Hugo had written at Oxford, a play full of soaring, impossible romanticism. But that had been a long time ago, when Hugo had been going to be the world's greatest playwright, when he had been in love with Alice, when he'd been on a permanent high.

As he returned with the drinks, Hugo was patently not on a high. He looked ill at ease, vulnerable, potentially petulant.

The rehearsal room was beginning to fill up now, as the stars of the Backstagers emerged in their party finery. Charles was relieved to see they all got the same vinegary reception from Reggie at the bar. (Maybe he had made the mistake of trying the wine.)

Hugo seemed to know many of the people who came in. Though not involved in the acting side, he was a regular of the Back Room, using it as his local, often dropping in for a drink on his way home from work. He dished out some abrupt nods and deterrent smiles to acquaintances, but seemed anxious to stay with Charles. It was reminiscent of parties in their first terms at Oxford, staying together shy against the wall until they had had enough to drink to risk a social foray.

A young man in jeans and a denim shirt came over to them. His face still glowed with the scrubbing it had taken to remove the make-up and there were streaks of grease-paint behind his ears. Charles recognized him from the stage, where less than half an hour before he had gone out to shoot himself in the character of Konstantin. In his own character, he didn't look suicidal. Cocky would be a better word. A handsome young face, pulled out of true by lines of arrogance around the mouth.

"Hugo! How'd you like it?" He must have been nearly thirty years younger, but the tone was patronizing.

"Fine." Hugo was unexpansive.

"Little lady did well."

Hugo flicked a one-frame smile across his face.

Konstantin looked speculatively at Charles. Then, deciding that Hugo was not going to introduce them, he reached out a man-of-the-world hand. "I'm Clive Steele."

"Charles Paris."

"Thought you must be. Charlie said the old man was bringing you." Charles felt Hugo stiffen. Difficult to tell whether it was at his wife's nickname or his own designation. The boy continued with a self-deprecating smile. "Well, how did it seem to you, Charles? How did the stumbling efforts of the amateurs seem to you as a professional theatre man?"

The boy was not really asking his opinion; he was fishing for compliments. Charles didn't know whether to give a vague reassurance as he would to any professional actor after a performance or to do exactly as he had been asked and give professional criticism. It was something he was going to have to sort out before the Critics' Circle on the Tuesday.

He made some trimming remark about the show with an ambiguous comment on Clive's performance. It was a waste of ambiguity; Clive took it as a straight compliment.

The conversation eddied. Clive, unprompted, but assuming its unfailing interest, provided his life story. He was becoming an accountant. The next week he had to go to Melton Mowbray on an audit. All bloody week. He had done a lot of productions with the Breckton Backstagers, mostly leads.

Charles couldn't resist it. "Yes, amateur dramatic societies are always hard-up for young men."

But Clive was well armored with self-opinion. "Certainly for ones who can act and are anything like decent-looking."

Charles didn't bother any more. The conversation was nearly dead, now he had withdrawn. But the boy kept talking. Like Hugo, Clive didn't seem to want to leave this particular corner. They both seemed to be waiting for something. Charles wondered if it was Charlotte.

A new couple came over and gave the conversation the kiss of life. This time Hugo remembered his social graces. "This is Charles Paris. Charles, Denis and Mary Hobbs."

"Oh dear," Mary giggled, "you're the one who's going to pass judgement on our performance. Now I do hope you'll treat us just like professionals."

It took him a minute or two to place her. She looked so different in the turquoise trouser suit, orange silk blouse and rainbow lamé slippers. And the blonded hair and too-young make-up. But when he added a rust-colored pre-Revolutionary Russian dress and a high-piled black wig. . . . "Of course. Madame Arkadina. I'm so sorry. I just didn't recognize you."

Yes, he was full of admiration for her make-up. On her performance he hoped he wouldn't be drawn. That kind of criticism could well wait till the Tuesday. In spite of himself, he found he was forming phrases of his real critical opinion. Such a pity that amateurs are always tempted by classic plays. Just because they're classics, it doesn't mean they're easy to do. In fact, often just the reverse. Arkadina is one of the great rôles of the theatre and not to be handed out at random to anyone who happened to have recited nicely at the Women's Institute Concert. Amateurs should stick to what's within their range—Agatha Christies, frothy West End comedies, nothing that involves too much subtlety of characterization. Leave Chekhov to the professionals.

Good God, there were only two people in that cast

tonight who got within a mile of what it was about—Charlotte as Nina and the guy who played Trigorin. The rest should take up something else to fill their evenings—like stamp-collecting.

Even as he framed the thoughts, he knew he was over-reacting. It was the irrational but instinctive response of anyone who made his living by acting. The very existence of amateur dramatic societies seemed to cast doubt on the seriousness of his profession.

Mary Hobbs was in full theatrical spate. "Oh God, there was a terrible moment in the first act, when we were meant to be watching Konstantin's play and I had this line about there being a smell of sulphur, and I think one of the stage managers had brought some fish and chips into the wings, because suddenly we all got this amazing whiff of vinegar across the stage, and I caught Geoff's eye and I'm afraid I just went. Total, absolute corpse. I turned upstage. I don't know if anyone noticed in the audience..."

Charles had noticed. Any experienced actor would have been aware of the tell-tale snort and sudden movement. And how typical of the Backstagers that they should have all the theatrical slang. A "corpse" was a breakdown into laughter on stage.

Mary Hobbs appealed to her husband. "Did you notice it, Den?"

"Blimey, no. Couldn't take my eyes off your missus, Hugo. I didn't see much else, eh?"

He erupted with laughter. Not particularly amused laughter, just the sort that some hearty people use around their speech like quotation marks.

The reactions to his remark were interesting. Hugo grimaced in an irritated way, as if he didn't want to be reminded of Charlotte's existence. Mary Hobbs flashed a look of reproof which quelled her husband. He looked like a schoolboy who had spoken out of turn, gauche as if he shouldn't have said anything in his rough voice while his wife was present to elocute for the two of them.

Mary's admonition was over in a second and she resumed her theatrical reminiscence. "Of course, Geoffrey didn't break up. He is marvellous. Didn't you think he was marvellous, Charles? Geoffrey Winter, our Trigorin. He's so clever. We really all think he ought to go on the stage professionally. He's so much better than most professional actors you see on the telly-box."

Charles didn't know whether this was meant to be deliberately rude, but let it pass. Mary Hobbs didn't seem to need reaction to impel her dialogue. She sighed dramatically. "Oh, It's all over. *Quelle tristesse.*"

"Till the next one." Denis supplied her cue promptly, as if to make up for his earlier faux pas.

"Till the next one. *Winter's Tale.* Dear old Shakespeare. Start rehearsing next week."

There was a moment of silence and Hugo seemed to wake up to some sort of social duty. But his question showed he had not been listening to the conversation. "Now the show's over, Denis, will you be able to get some weekends down at the cottage?"

Denis gave his punctuation of laughter. "Yes, not before time. I must say we've been living Chekhov this last couple of months. And what with all the Sunday afternoon rehearsals, we only got away one weekend since August."

"Still we are going away this weekend." Again the edge of reproof in his wife's voice.

Denis compensated quickly. "Oh yes. It's just one of the penalties of marrying talent, eh?" Another unmotivated eruption. Mary smiled and he reckoned he could risk a little joke. "She's spent so much time here recently I kept saying why didn't she move in? After all, we're only next door." This too was apparently very funny.

Mary graciously allowed him this little indulgence and then felt it was time to draw attention to her magnanimity. "Still, this weekend I'm going to make it all up to you, aren't I?" She took her husband's hand and patted it with a coquettishness which Charles found unattractive in a woman in her fifties. "First thing in the morning, when all the rest of the naughty Backstagers are sleeping off their hangovers, we'll be in the new Rover sweeping off down to the cottage for a little delayed weekend. All tomorrow, and all Monday—well, till nine or so when we'll drive back. Just the two of us. A second honeymoon—or is it a third?"

"Three hundredth," said Denis, which was the cue for another explosion of merriment.

Charles escaped to get more drinks. Soon the wine would cease to taste of anything and his bad temper would begin to dissipate.

While he queued at sour Reggie's bar, he looked around at the kindling party. There was music now, music rather younger than the average age of those present. But the pounding beat was infectious.

As the room filled, he was increasingly aware of the common complaint of amateur dramatic societies—that there are always more women than men. And some of them were rather nice. He felt a little glow of excitement. No one knew him down in Breckton. It was like being given a whole new copybook to blot.

Some couples were dancing already. Charlotte Mecken was out there, with her arms around Clive Steele. They were moving together sensuously to the slow pounding of the music. But what they were doing was paradoxically not sexy. It had the air of a performance, as if they were still on stage, as if their closeness was for the benefit of the audience, not because it expressed any real mutual attraction.

The same could be said of the Trigorin, Geoffrey Winter. He was dancing with a pretty young girl, whose paint-spattered jeans suggested she was one of the stage staff. They were not dancing close, but in a jerky slow motion pantomime. Geoffrey moved well, his body flicking in time to the music, like a puppet out of control. But again it was a performance of a body out of control, not genuine abandon. Each movement was carefully timed; it was well-done, but calculated.

Charles had noticed the same quality in the man's stage performance. It had been enormously skilful and shown more technique than the rest of the cast put together, but it had been mannered and ultimately artificial, a performance from the head rather than the heart.

The man was good-looking in an angular way. Very thin, with grey hair and pale eyes. He wore a black shirt, black cord jeans and desert boots. There was something commanding about him, attractive in not just the physical sense of the word.

As Charles watched he saw the man change partners and start a new dance with another little totty. "Enjoying himself, isn't he?"

He turned to the owner of the voice which had spoken beside him. A young woman of about thirty. Short mousy hair, wide green eyes. Attractive. She was following Charles's gaze towards the dancing Trigorin. "My husband."

She said it wryly. Not bitterly or critically, but just as if it were a fact that ought to be established.

"Ah. I'm Charles Paris."

"Thought you must be." Charles felt the inevitable actor's excitement that she was going to say she recognized him from the television. But no. "You're the only person down here I didn't recognize. And I knew you'd be in tonight because you're doing the crit on Tuesday, so, by a process of elimination...."

"I'm Vee Winter, by the way. Though I act here under my maiden name, Vee le Carpentier. I always think if people see in programmes that the leads are played by people with the same surname, they get to think the Backstagers are awfully cliquey." Before Charles had time to take in this statement, she went on, "Have you met Geoffrey?"

"No, just seen him on stage. He's very talented." Charles didn't volunteer whether he thought the talent was being appropriately used.

"Yes, he's talented." She changed the subject abruptly. "Since you're coming down to do this thing on Tuesday, why not have a meal with us beforehand?"

"That's very kind," said Charles, wondering if he ought to check whether Hugo and Charlotte were expecting him.

Vee took it as assent. "About half-past seven. The Critics' Circle isn't till eight-thirty. I'll give you our phone number in case you have problems."

"Fine." Charles made a note of the number. Then he added, because he was beginning to understand suburban timetables, "Seven-thirty then. After the children are asleep."

"We don't have any children," said Vee Winter.

Sour Reggie dispensed Charles's order for drinks as if the country were threatened by imminent drought. Vee helped carry the glasses back to the group.

She seemed to know them all. She made some insincere compliment to Mary Hobbs about her Arkadina.

"Oh, that's sweet of you to say so, darling. Actually..." The voice dropped with the subtlety of a double declutch on a worn gear-box. "...I still think you would have made a better Nina, but, you know, Shad gets these ideas...."

The circle had enlarged in Charles's absence to include an elderly man with a white goatee beard. And Hugo's mood had shifted into something more expansive. "Charles, I don't think you've met Robert Chubb. Bob, this is Charles Paris. Bob's the founder of the whole set-up. Started the Backstagers back in...ooh...."

"Nineteen hundred and mind-your-own-business," supplied Robert Chubb jovially. "First productions in the Church Hall, mind you. Come some way since then. Started the fund for this complex in 1960... and ten years later it was all finished." He gestured to the rehearsal room and theatre.

It was an impressive achievement. Charles bit back his cynical views on the subject of amateur theatre and said so.

Robert Chubb seemed to have been waiting for this cue to launch into the next instalment of his monologue. "Well, I thought, I and a few like-minded cronies, that there should be some decent theatre in Breckton. I mean, it's so easy for people in the suburbs to completely lose sight of culture.

"So we damned well worked to set up something good—not just your average amateur dramatic society, performing your Agatha Christies and your frothy West End comedies, but a society with high professional standards, which kept in touch with what was happening in the theatre at large. And that's how the Backstagers started."

Charles felt he was being addressed like a television interviewer who had actually asked for this potted history. And his interviewee continued. "And now it's grown like this. Enormous membership, great waiting list of people from all over South London keen to join in the fun. Lots of Press coverage—particularly for our World Premières Festival.

"It just keeps getting bigger. Now we run our own fort-nightly newsletter to keep people informed of what we're up to— called *Backchat*, don't know if you've seen it?"

"No."

"Then of course this bar's called the Back Room."

"I see, everthing's Back-something-or-other?"

"Yes. Rather nice, isn't it?"

Charles's mind began seething with new permutations of Back-, most of them obscene. It was perhaps as well that Hugo spoke before he launched into any of them. "We must get Charles down here to do a production, eh, Bob?"

It was Charles's turn to be self-deprecating. "Oh, come on, Hugo, I'm a professional actor. Much as I'd like to do it, I'm likely to be off touring or something at a moment's notice."

"Nonsense. This voice-over campaign's really going to take off. You'll be stuck in London with more work than you can cope with."

"When that happens—" Charles joked, "and I won't believe it until it does—I'll be prepared to do a production for the Backstagers." That seemed to get him safely off the hook.

But a new voice joined the circle and qualified his remark. "If, of course, you do a successful One-Act Productions Audition and your choice of play is approved by the Directorial Selection Sub-Committee." Charles was not surprised to find that the voice came from sour Reggie, the walking rule-book.

"Oh, Charles has had rather a lot of experience as a director." It was Hugo coming to his rescue. Charles didn't want rescuing. He thought doing a production for the Breckton Backstagers was a consummation devoutly to be avoided. The atmosphere was getting claustrophobic.

But Hugo's defence was quite impassioned. Again Charles was conscious of the other man's need for him. He was being paraded for the benefit of Hugo's local crowd. In a strange way, it seemed to tie in with Charlotte's behavior, as if Hugo's ignoring his wife was justified by the fact that he had a genuine professional actor to show off.

Charles was being used and he didn't like it, but Hugo continued with his sales campaign. "Charles is a bit of a playwright too. You should get him to write something for the World Premières Festival."

Charles made some suitably modest response, but Robert Chubb seized on the cue. "Oh really, if you've got something that hasn't been performed tucked away in a cupboard, do let us see it. We're getting the next Festival sorted out at the moment and one of our expected scripts has just fallen through, so we'd be very interested."

Charles was tempted. There was in fact an unperformed play sitting in a drawer in his room in Hereford Road. He'd written it after his one successful play, *The Ratepayer*. A light comedy, called *How's Your Father?* It would be quite gratifying to have it done under any circumstances.

But the patronising tone in which Robert Chubb continued changed his mind. "It could do you a lot of good, Charles. Lots of plays we've premiered here have gone on to do awfully well. It's a real chance for an unknown playwright. I don't know if you know George Walsh's *Doomwomb*?"

Charles shook his head. Robert Chubb smiled indulgently at his ignorance. "That started here."

"Really?" Suddenly he wanted to scream, wanted to do something appalling, be very rude to someone, break something, get the hell away from all these pretentious idiots.

Rescue came from an unexpected source. He felt an arm round his waist and a female body pressed close to his. "Dance with me."

It was Vee Winter.

Two...

SHE WAS A strange woman. She clung to him tightly and he could feel the nervous excitement coursing through her body. In other circumstances, he would have interpreted this as a sexual message and responded in kind, but that somehow didn't seem appropriate. The excitement had nothing to do with him.

He was being used for some purpose of her own. Certainly she was working to give the appearance of a sexual encounter, but it was for the benefit of the rest of the room, not for her partner.

Charles wondered at first if it was a ploy to make her husband jealous. Geoffrey was across the room, dancing with circumscribed abandon in front of yet another little dolly and Vee was very aware of his presence. But her behaviour did not seem designed to antagonize him; instead Charles received an inexplicable impression of complicity between husband and wife, as if their performances were co-ordinated parts of an overall plan and would later be laughed over when they were alone together.

This annoyed him. Again he was being used as a counter in a game he didn't understand. The heavy beat of a rock number changed to a soupy ballad and Vee snuggled closer, pressing the contours of her body tightly against his. He realised with surprise that he didn't find this arousing. Vee Winter was an attractive woman, but he didn't fancy her. This gave him a perverse sense of righteousness, as if confirming that his randiness was not absolutely indiscriminate.

He commented rather coldly on her forwardness. "Is this to give food for scandal to the gossip columnist of *Backbite*?"

"*Backbite*?"

"Your fortnightly magazine."

"That's called *Backchat*." She corrected him without humor. "Anyway, it doesn't have a gossip columnist."

Charles unwisely chose to continue in facetious vein. "So there's no one to chronicle the backslidings of the Backstagers bopping to Burt Bacharach and their bacchanalian orgies?"

"No." Vee's reply was absolutely straight. Charles wouldn't have minded if she had said it as a put-down (his attempt at humor had been pretty feeble), but for her not to notice even that the attempt had been made, that he found galling.

"Do you act much here?"

She laughed with incredulity at his question, rather as if someone had asked the Queen if she had any jewelery. "Oh, I have done a few things, yes."

"But not *The Seagull*?"

"No." She stiffened slightly. "I really felt I needed a rest. Also I've played so many leads in the past year, I didn't want it to look as if Geoff and I were monopolizing the entire society. Ought to give some of the newer members a chance. And then Shad, who directed, had this strange notion that Nina ought to have red hair. He's a rather quirky director, if you know what I mean."

Through the excuses, Charles knew exactly what she meant.

*   *   *

He took the end of a record as an opportunity to end their clinch. He looked over at the group round Hugo and couldn't face it yet. He needed just to get out of the place for a moment. The sweet wine was making him feel sick. Pausing only to pick up someone's full glass off a table, he left the rehearsal room.

The change was as welcome as he had anticipated. In spite of the summery days of that fall, October was nearing its end and the evenings were chilly. The slap of cold air was refreshing. He leaned against the inside of the porch and breathed deeply.

Then he heard the voices. Charlotte Mecken and Clive Steele. Arguing in fierce whispers. First Charlotte's voice, the veneer of drama school thinned by emotion to reveal its Northern Irish origin. "... I'm sorry, Clive, you've got it completely wrong. I never knew you were thinking that."

"What was I meant to think, after all those rehearsals, when you suddenly got all emotional and confided in me when I drove you home?"

"I'm sorry. I shouldn't have broken down. I just ... it was all too much. ..."

"Well, I made the perfectly natural assumption that—"

"It may have seemed perfectly natural to you, but—"

"It bloody well did. Look, if it's your husband you're worried about, forget it. It's bloody obscene you being married to him anyway. Reminds me of all those jokes about young girls on their wedding nights feeling old age creeping all over them—"

"Clive, stop it. You've got the wrong end of the stick. So completely the wrong end. It's all much more complicated than you can begin to imagine. Look, I'm sorry if you've been hurt, but I can assure you—"

"Oh, stuff that! All right, you've made your point. I see what's been happening now. There is a word for women who lead men on, you know."

"Clive, if I'd had any idea of what was going through your mind—"

"Oh shut up. I'm going."

"Be careful."

"Don't worry, I will. I'm not like Konstantin—I'm not going to go off and shoot myself because some tart's let me down. If I were to do anything, I can assure you it would be something a lot more practical. Goodbye!"

Charles heard a few brisk footsteps across the gravel, a car door open and slam, then a powerful sports car engine starting and tires screeching off down the road.

He assumed Charlotte was still there. He gave her two minutes, then, not being an actor for nothing, did his impression of someone coming noisily out of the rehearsal room.

He was aware of her perfume before he saw her. It was very expensive, very distinctive. Whatever Hugo's relationship with his wife, he didn't stint her expenses. Her clothes were also of the best. She was a trendy fashion plate amidst the pervading dowdiness of the Backstagers.

She was leaning against the bonnet of a Volvo in the car park and didn't look as if she had moved for some time. Her face was infinitely miserable.

"Hello, Charlotte. What's up?"

"I don't know. Last night blues," she lied. "You should understand about that."

"Yes. What I usually do is get wildly pissed. Then I don't notice. And the next morning I feel so bad physically that I forget about any emotional upset."

"Hmm. I'm rather off alcohol at the moment."

Silence. She looked sensational in the bluish light shed from the rehearsal room. The pain of her expression increased rather than diminished her beauty. The face framed in red hair looked pale and peaky in the thin light. Very young, very vulnerable, a child being brave.

Charles found being with her a relief. She seemed more like a real person than the lot in the rehearsal room. He felt protective towards her. And that made him feel better.

He didn't like the boorish bloody-mindedness which the massed Backstagers kindled in him.

"You know, your Nina was very good."

"Thank you. What are you going to say—I ought to take it up professionally?"

"That's what you were trained for."

"Yes. A bit pathetic, isn't it really—fully trained actress mucking about with amateur dramatics."

"Oh, I don't know. I'm sure, if you pass your Juvenile Lead Audition and are approved by the Big Parts Selection Sub-Committee, you'll get some very juicy roles here."

Charlotte laughed. "You seem to have caught on to the atmosphere of the place very quickly. God, what a load of creeps they all seem when you think of them objectively. All with their oversize egos and silly stage names—all those abbreviations and hyphens and extra middle names— it makes me sick when I think about it. I make a point of using their proper names just to annoy them."

"Do you think you'll do more here?"

"Maybe. I don't know. What's the alternative? I can't see Hugo being keen on my having a real acting career. Anyway, I've lost all the few contacts I ever had in the theatre. Just a housewife with dreams, I suppose."

"I'm sure you could make it in the real theatre."

"'You should go on the stage,' says Arkadina. 'Yes, that is my one dream,' replies Nina. 'But it'll never come true.'"

"Could do."

But Charlotte's temporary serenity was broken by some memory. "No, it'll never—oh, everything's such a mess. God knows what's in store for me anyway."

"Anything you can talk about?"

She hesitated for a moment, on the verge of sharing her burden. But decided against it. "No. Thanks for the offer, but I'm rather against shoulders to cry on at the moment. It's my own mess and I must sort it out somehow." She moved resolutely away from the Volvo.

"Are you coming back in, Charlotte?"

"No, I can't face that lot right now. I'm just going to . . . I don't know . . . have a bit of a walk, try to clear my head or . . . I don't know, Charles. Tell Hugo I'll be back later. You're staying with us tonight, aren't you?"

"If that's okay."

"Sure. I'll see you in the morning." She walked off into the night, pulling her long Aran cardigan round her against the cold.

Hugo had been hard at the Spanish red when Charles got back into the rehearsal room. But the mood that was settling in was one of catatonic gloom rather than manic violence.

They both continued to drink, resolutely and more or less silently. The party was livening up, with more and more couples clinched on the dance-floor. There were still plenty of spare women, but Charles had lost interest. The intensity of Vee Winter and Charlotte's troubled words had changed his mood. He and Hugo drank as they might have done thirty years earlier at an Oxford party where all the women had been bagged before they arrived.

It was about three when they left. Charles murmured something about Charlotte making her own way home, but Hugo didn't react. He drove them back to his house with the punctilious concentration of the very drunk.

As the Alfa-Romeo saloon crunched to a halt on the gravel in front of the house, he said determinedly. "Come in and have a nightcap."

Charles didn't want to. He was tired and drunk and he had a potentially difficult day ahead of him. Also he had a premonition that Hugo wanted to confide in him. Ignobly, he didn't feel up to it.

But Hugo took his silence for assent and they went into the sitting room. Charles stood with his back to the empty fireplace, trying to think of a good line to get him quickly up to bed, while Hugo went over to the drinks cupboard. "What's it to be?"

He opened the door to reveal a neat parade of whisky bottles. There were up to a dozen brands. Hugo always rationalized the size of the display on the grounds that everyone has a favorite Scotch, but it was really just the potential alcoholic's insurance policy.

Charles missed the opportunity to refuse and weakly chose a Glenmorangie malt. Hugo poured a generous two inches into a tumbler and helped himself to a Johnnie Walker Black Label.

Then they just stood facing each other and drank. Hugo kept the Johnnie Walker bottle dangling in his free hand. The silence became oppressive. Charles downed his drink in a few long swallows and opened his mouth for thank you and goodnight.

Hugo spoke first. "Charles," he said in a voice of uneven pitch, "I think I'm cracking up."

"What do you mean?"

"Cracking up, going round the bend, *losing control*." The last two words came out in a fascinated whisper.

"Oh come on, you're pissed."

"That's part of it. I drink too much and I just don't notice it. It doesn't make me drunk, it doesn't calm me down, I just feel the same thing—that I'm... losing control."

"Control of what? What do you think you are going to do?"

"I don't know. Something terrible. I'm going to say something awful, hit somebody or.... All the constraints I've built up over the years, they're just breaking down...I...." He mouthed incoherently.

"Oh come on. You've just had too much to drink. It's nothing."

"Don't tell me it's nothing!" Hugo suddenly screamed. As he did so, he hurled the whisky bottle at the stone mantelpiece to the right of Charles. It shattered. Glass fell into the fireplace and spirit dripped down on to it.

Charles thought the outburst contained more than a dash of histrionics. If his friend wasn't going to believe him, then Hugo was damned well going to give a demonstration of his lack of control. "Like that, you mean?" asked Charles. "Out of control like that?"

Hugo looked at him defiantly, then sheepishly, then with a hint of a smile, seeing that his bluff had been called. He sank exhausted into a chair. "No, not like that. That was just for effect. I mean worse than that. I get to a flashpoint and I feel I'm going to lash out—I don't know, to kill someone."

Charles looked straight at him and Hugo looked away, again slightly sheepish, admitting that the homicidal threat was also for effect.

"Who are you going to kill?" Charles teased. "Charlotte?"

Hugo was instantly serious. "No, not Charlotte. I wouldn't touch Charlotte. Whatever she did, I wouldn't touch her."

"Then who?"

Hugo looked at Charles vaguely, distantly, as if piecing together something that had only just occurred to him. Then he said slowly, as if he didn't believe it, "Friends of Charlotte."

Charles took a risk and laughed. Hugo looked at him suspiciously for a moment and then laughed too. Soon after they went to bed.

Charles didn't think too much about what Hugo had said. Obviously his friend was under pressure and all wasn't well with his marriage, but most of the trouble was the drink.

Anyway, Charles had domestic problems of his own to worry about. His last thought, before he dropped into the alcohol-anaesthetized sleep which was becoming too much of a habit, was the next day he had to see his wife for the first time in five months. At the christening of their twin grandsons. Grandsons, for God's sake.

Three...

THE CHRISTENING WENT okay, he supposed. Difficult to say, really It was a long time since he had been to one with which to compare it. The twins were healthy five-month-old boys and they were successfully received into the Church of England in Pangbourne in Berkshire, which was where Charles's daughter Juliet and her husband Miles (who was apparently carving a successful career for himself in insurance) lived. The boys were named Damian and Julian, which would not have been their grandfather's choice.

So everything went as it should have done. But it was not an easy day for Charles. Being with Frances and behaving as if they were still conventional man and wife had been strange. In some ways seductively appealing. His mind was still full of the bourgeois morality of Breckton and he found himself wondering whether it could have worked, he and Frances as a couple, growing old together, building a family, having Juliet and the kids over for Sunday lunch and so on.

But deep down he knew that he'd followed the only

course open to him when he'd left Frances in 1961. He still loved her, still often would rather spend time with her than anyone else, but he never wanted to get back into the claustrophobia of always being there, always being answerable.

In a way, his leaving her had been as romantic as Hugo's leaving of Alice. But, unlike Hugo, Charles hadn't thought it was all possible, that a new woman could make it all all right again. He had left so as to keep some illusions. He didn't want just to sink into a middle age of disappointed bickering. Nor did he want to feel guilty if he had affairs with other women.

Of course, it hadn't worked. Guilt had remained in some form in all his affairs and much of the time he had been just lonely. But his single state gave him a kind of perverse integrity.

The situation had been complicated when it transpired that Frances had developed some sort of boyfriend. Charles never knew how serious the relationship was. The only thing he did know was that, illogically, it made him jealous.

And so, even more illogically, did seeing Frances so wrapped up in the twins. He felt excluded, as he had when she had been pregnant with Juliet.

That was the trouble. Whenever he saw Frances, unwelcome emotional confusion crowded into his mind. When he didn't see her, he could exist quite happily from moment to moment, without thinking all the time that feelings had to be defined and formalized.

At the christening he hardly saw her. It was a public occasion, there were other people there, he had no real chance to ask her the sort of questions he wanted to. Or felt he ought to.

He went through it all in the train on the way back to London. He must ring Frances—soon. They must meet and talk, really talk.

The day had increased the unease which the atmosphere between Hugo and Charlotte had fomented in him.

He tried to think if there was anything comforting that had emerged. Only the fact that his son-in-law Miles, Mr. Prudent, king of the insurance world, with a policy for every hazard, had not insured against twins.

The Monday recording session was for a series of radio commercials, which was much less hairy than the voice-to-picture session which had preceded it. All Charles had to do was to read some copy in the same voice that he had used in the television commercials.

Not very hard work. And well spread out. Even this simple job was to be done in two sessions: half of the commercials were to be recorded the following Tuesday morning.

The whole voice-over business still puzzled him. Giving a couple of dozen readings of a banal endorsement for some product which no self-respecting housewife should be without didn't fit into his definition of acting.

Still, the money was good, potentially very good. And it was different. And so long as one didn't take it too seriously, it was better than sitting at home waiting for the telephone to ring.

It had started out of the blue some two months before with a bewildered call from his agent, Maurice Skellern. Someone from Mills Brown Mazzini had been enquiring about Charles Paris's availability for voice-over work. That had led to a series of in-house voice tests in a tatty studio at the advertising agency.

Presumably (though no one ever actually told him so) these had been successful, because within a week he had been summoned to a session of voice-to-picture tests. These had been more elaborate, in a swish professional dubbing theatre, and attended by an enormous gallery of advertising people, all of whom, it seemed, had the right to give him notes on his performance.

Again (though nobody actually said so) he must have been successful, because soon after he was summoned to put his voice to three television commercials, which were apparently on test transmission in the Tyne-Tees area.

It was Hugo Mecken he had to thank for this new development in his acting career. It seemed that Hugo had secured the account for a new bedtime drink which was being launched by a huge Dutch-owned drugs company. The drink was to be called Bland and the campaign had been agreed on some months before. It was to be led by a cartoon character called Mr. Bland who wore a top-hat and tails. In the launching series of animated television commercials he was to visit a tribe of little fuzzy red creatures called the Wideawakes. When presented with cups of Bland on a silver salver by Mr. Bland, they gradually turned pale blue and fell asleep. Over their snoring, Mr. Bland intoned the words, "Bland soothes away the day."

The voice of Mr. Bland, which, if the campaign took off as it was hoped, would be a very lucrative assignment, had gone to Christopher Milton, a well-known stage and television actor (who, apart from his current success in the musical *Lumpkin!* at the King's Theatre, was said by Hugo recently to have signed a contract for £25,000 to do an in-vision commercial for instant coffee).

All this had been agreed with the Brand Manager for Bland, the animation voice-track was recorded and the animation work was started. From which point all should have gone well until the launching of the product.

But during the interval between the agreement of the campaign and the completion of the three test commercials the Brand Manager for Bland had been appointed European Marketing Manager for the huge Dutch-owned drugs company. His successor on Bland, a Mr. Farrow, saw the commericals and, as a matter of principle, didn't like them. Because of the proximity of the launch date and because of the enormous cost of the animation, he couldn't afford to make radical changes in the campaign. So he homed in on the voice.

It was totally wrong, he cried. Far too patronizing, too light, it didn't treat the product seriously enough, suggested that the whole sales campaign was a bit of a joke. Hugo and his associates held back their view that little fuzzy red figures called Wideawakes were not going to look very serious however funereal the voice that addressed them and said yes, of course he was right and they had rather suspected this might be a problem from the start and they'd go straight off and find another voice.

By coincidence, on the very evening of the meeting at which this decision had been made, Charles Paris was appearing in a television play. It was one of the few jobs he had had in a very lean year and he was playing an avuncular Victorian solicitor. His voice was somewhat deeper than usual because he had had a cold at the time of the recording.

Whether it was this odd voice quality or the fact that he had worn tailcoat and top-hat that made him seem to Hugo to be the ideal Mr. Bland, Charles never knew. Secretly he thought it was partly that Hugo knew that he would be easy to work with and that the Creative Director desperately needed to come up with something new. It was evident that Hugo, in a business that thrives on ideas, was beginning to run out of them.

He could feel the pressure from the inventive minds of younger copywriters and the task of finding the new voice for Mr. Bland was a competitive issue in the agency. There were other members of the staff with other candidates and the results of the voice-to-picture tests could well cause some realignment in the creative hierarchy of Mills Brown Mazzini.

So when the new Bland Brand Manager, Mr. Farrow, chose Charles Paris from the tests, Hugo was over the moon. It was then that he had started the showing off and parading of his new discovery which had so annoyed Charles at the Backstagers' party.

(For Charles the success was not without irony, because it involved getting one up on Christopher Milton, whose path he had crossed during the accident-haunted rehearsals for the musical *Lumpkin!*)

● ● ●

Charles was now familiar with the small commercial recording studio where he was to work. Through the glossy foyer with its low glass desks and low oatmeal couches, downstairs to the tiny Studio Two.

God knows what the building had been before conversion. A private house maybe, with the studio as a larder. The conversion had consisted mainly of sticking cork tiles on every available surface. In spite of the expensive recording hardware, the whole operation looked unfinished and temporary, as if all the cork could be stripped off and the studio equipment dismantled in half an hour so that the real owner would never know what his premises had been used for during his absence.

Hugo and Farrow were already sitting in the control cubicle. Hugo looked tired and nervous.

They started recording. The copy was so similar to the television version that any notes on performance given in those sessions were still applicable, but Farrow was determined to give them all again. Like all Brand Managers (indeed it is an essential qualification for the job), he was without artistic judgement.

Charles had now done enough of these sessions to know how to behave. Just take it, do as you're told even if it's wrong, don't comment, don't suggest, above all don't try to put any of yourself into it. The agency and, indirectly, the client had hired his voice as a piece of machinery, and it was their right to use it as they thought fit, even if the owner of the machinery knew it wasn't being used in the best way. At worst, there was the comfort that the session was only booked for an hour and he was being paid for it. Thirty-five quid basic, with possible repeats.

So, with his voice lowered an octave to recapture the coldy quality of his Victorian solicitor, Charles gave every possible reading of the lines. He hit each word in turn to satisfy Farrow. BLAND soothes away the day. Bland SOOTHES away the day. Bland soothes AWAY the day.

Bland.... It did seem a rather pointless exercise for a grown man.

Within half an hour all possible inflections of the lines had been recorded and Charles went from the studio into the control cubicle. Farrow was still not happy. After some deliberation, he pronounced, "I think it may not be the actor's fault this time." Charles found that charming. "No, I think it's the copy that's wrong."

Hugo's voice was extremely reasonable as he replied. "But you have already passed the copy as suitable for the television commercials, and I thought the idea was to keep the two the same."

"If so, the idea was wrong," said Farrow accusingly.

"Well, it was your bloody idea," Hugo suddenly snapped.

Farrow looked at him in amazement, as if he must have misheard. In times when there was so much competition for big accounts, no member of an agency would dare to disagree with a client. After a pause, he continued as though Hugo had not spoken. "I'm afraid you advised us wrongly on that. The radio campaign must be entirely rethought. I can see it's easy for you to use the same copy, but I'm not the sort of man to take short cuts. I care about this product and I'm looking for a campaign that's going to be both effective from the sales point of view and also artistically satisfying."

This was too much for Hugo. "Christ, now I've heard it all. Artistically satisfying—what the hell do you know what's artistically satisfying? I've listened to enough crap from you and all the other jumped-up little commercial travellers who try to tell me how to do my job. Stick to what you're good at—peddling pap to the masses—and leave me to get on with what I'm good at—making advertising."

There was a long pause. Mr. Farrow collected together his papers and put them in his briefcase. Had he left the room in silence, it could have been a dignified exit. But he let it down by trying an exit line. "More powerful men than you, Mr. Mecken, have tried to beat me and failed."

This, delivered in his nasal London whine was suddenly unaccountably funny, and Charles and Hugo both erupted with laughter almost before the door had closed behind the aggrieved Brand Manager.

Hugo's laughter was a short, nervous burst and when it had passed, he looked ghastly, drained of color. "Oh shit, I shouldn't have done it. I'll have to go after him and apologize. I wasn't thinking—or I was thinking about other things. I just snapped."

He rose to leave. Suddenly Charles was worried about him. He couldn't forget their drunken conversation on the Saturday night. The outburst against Farrow had sounded like an overdue expression of home truths, but now he wondered if it had been a more fundamental breakdown of control.

Hugo stood dazed for a moment and then started for the door. "I've booked a table at the Trattoria for twelve-thirty. See you there. I'll get along as soon as I can."

Four...

CHARLES WALKED ROUND Soho until it was time
to go to the restaurant for another expense account meal.
He gave Hugo's name and was shown to a table where
there were already two young men.

One he recognized as Ian Compton, a bright
copy-writer of about twenty-four who was under Hugo at
Mills Brown Mazzini. He was wearing a double-breasted
ganster-striped suit over a pale blue T-shirt. Around his
neck hung a selection of leather thongs, one for a biro, one
for a packet of Gauloise, one for a Cricket lighter and
others whose function was not immediately apparent. His
lapels bristled with badges, gollies, teddy bears, a spilling
tomato ketchup bottle and similar trendy kitsch.

The other was more soberly dressed in a dark jacket
and open-necked brown shirt. "Diccon, this is Charles
Paris. I told you about him." Ian's tone implied that what
he had told hadn't been wholly enthusiastic. "This is
Diccon Hudson."

"Hello." The name rang a bell. Charles had heard

Diccon spoken of as one of the few who made a very good living exclusively from voice-over work.

Diccon looked at him appraisingly. Not rudely, just with great interest, sizing him up professionally. "So you're the guy who got the Mr. Bland campaign."

"'Fraid so," said Charles inanely.

"Oh, don't apologize. You win some, you lose some."

So Diccon had been one of his rivals for the job. Intuition told him that he was facing Ian Compton's candidate.

"Who's your agent?" asked Diccon suddenly.

"Maurice Skellern."

"Never heard of him." Was there a hint of relief in the voice? "You want a specialist voice-over agent if you're going to get anywhere in this business."

"Where's the old man?" asked Ian, as Charles ordered a Scotch.

"Hugo? Oh, he's . . . he'll be along shortly." Charles felt it prudent to keep quiet about the scene with Farrow.

It was Diccon's turn for a sudden question. "Do you know Charlotte?"

"Hugo's wife? Yes."

"How is she?" The inquiry was poised midway between solicitude and insolence.

"Fine." Not the moment to share her anxieties of the Saturday night. "You know her well?"

"Used to. Before she got married. Drama school together. Used to go around with her." There was a shading of sexual bravado in his tone. "Quite cut up when she went into the geriatric ward, I was."

Charles ignored the implied rudeness. "But now you've managed to forgive Hugo?"

Diccon looked at him very straight. "Well, he's work, isn't he, love?"

At that moment the subject of their conversation arrived. He was deathly pale. It was impossible to guess at the outcome of his interview with Mr. Farrow. He was in need of a drink. "Got a lot of catching up to do. Marcello, vodka and Campari for me, please. And the same again for the others."

Hugo started drinking as if he were trying to catch up on a whole lifetime. He became very jovial, swopping flip dialogue, scandal and crude anecdotes with the two young men in a way that was jarringly out of character. Charles didn't like the sight of Hugo being one of the boys. And he didn't like the way the two young men were responding to it either. Hugo didn't seem to notice the covert smiles that passed between Ian and Diccon, or the hint of mockery in their tones as they spoke to him. It was not just at home that Hugo had problems.

As the drink got through, he became increasingly like a salesman in a dirty joke. At one point he leaned nudgingly across to Diccon. "What do you say to that bit over there? Chick by the wine rack, eh? Lovely pair of tits."

"Not bad." Diccon gave a superior smile. He knew Hugo was making a fool of himself and was enjoying every minute of it.

"That's what women should be like," Hugo went on in drunken man-of-the-world style. "Nice firm little tits. Don't let 'em have children. Never have children. Not worth the effort. Little buggers don't give a damn about you and look what they do to their mothers—make 'em bloody sag, ruin their figures, stop 'em being sexy. That's what women should be about—they're meant just to give you a bloody good time in bed, that's all."

They had reached the coffee stage. Charles looked round desperately for a waiter to come and bring a bill. He couldn't bear to see Hugo destroying himself much longer.

Diccon Hudson leaned across the table and said to Hugo in a very sincere voice, "So I take it you and Charlotte won't be starting a family?"

"No chance. I've been through all that and it doesn't work."

"So you've managed to persuade her to go on the Pill. Funny, she always used to be against the idea."

Diccon's ambiguous indiscretion had been quite deliberate, but Hugo didn't rise to it. "Huh," he snorted, "there are other ways, you know. We didn't have any Pills in our young days, but we managed, didn't we, Charles? Eh, we managed."

Charles had had enough of this barrack-room talk. He rose. "I've got to be going now actually, Hugo."

"No, don't go." The appeal was naked, almost terrified. Charles sat down.

They left the Trattoria an interminable half-hour later, just after three. Diccon Hudson (who had drunk Perrier water throughout the meal) said he had to go off to his next recording session.

"They keep you busy," Charles observed and was rewarded by a complacent smile.

"Got an evening session tonight, have you, Diccon?" asked Ian in his usual insolent style.

Diccon colored. "No," he said and left without another word.

After Ian Compton had also gone, Charles turned to his friend. "Well, Hugo, thanks for the lunch. Look, I'll no doubt see you tomorrow down in Breckton for this Critics'—"

"Don't go, Charles. Let's have another drink. 'S a little club in Dean Street where I'm a member. C'mon, little quick one."

The club was a strip joint with gold chairs and a lot of hanging red velvet. A party of Japanese executives and a few morose single men watched a couple of girls playing with each other.

Hugo didn't seem to notice them. He ordered a bottle of Scotch. The boisterous, vulgar stage of drunkenness was now behind him; he settled down to silent, cold-blooded consumption.

Charles drank sparingly. He had the feeling that Hugo was going to need help before the day was out.

He tried asking what was the matter; he offered help.

"I don't want help, Charles, I don't want talk. I just want you to sit and bloody drink with me, that's all."

So they sat and bloody drank. Clients came and went. The girls were replaced by others who went through the same motions.

Eventually, Hugo seemed to relax. His eyelids flickered and his head started to nod. Charles looked at his watch and put his hand on his friend's arm. "Come on, it's nearly six. Let's go."

Hugo was surprisingly docile. He paid the bill (an amount which took Charles's breath away) without noticing. Out in the street he looked around blearily. "'S find a cab, Charles. Get the six-forty-two from Waterloo."

They were lucky to find one and got to the station in good time. Charles went off to buy a ticket and returned to find Hugo on the platform with a copy of the *Evening Standard* tucked under his arm. Charles made to move a little further down the platform. "No, Charles, here. Right opposite the barrier at Breckton."

Sure enough, twenty minutes later they got out of the train opposite the ticket collector. Hugo showed his season ticket with an unconscious reflex movement, turned right out of the station and started to walk along a footpath by the railway line. After a few steps he stopped.

"Come on, Hugo, let's get back to your place. See Charlotte."

"Charlotte." There was a deep misery in his echo.

"Yes. Come on."

"No." Hugo dithered like a recalcitrant two-year-old. "No, let's go up to the Backstagers and have a drink."

"Haven't we had enough drinks?" Charles spoke very gently.

"No, we bloody haven't! Don't you try to tell me when I've had enough!" Hugo bunched his fist and took a wild swing. Charles was able to block it harmlessly, but he felt the enormous strength of frustration in the blow.

Hugo went limp. "I'm sorry, Charles. I'm sorry. Silly.

Come on, come to the Backstagers—just for a quick one.
Often go there for a quick one on the way home."

"All right. A very quick one."

In the Back Room bar (manned that evening by Robert
Chubb) Hugo recommenced his silent, systematic drinking. Charles, himself no mean performer with a bottle,
was amazed at his friend's capacity. What made it
unnerving was the fact that after the outburst by the
station, it no longer seemed to have any effect. Hugo
spoke with great care, but without slurring. And still the
alcohol poured in, as if fuelling some inner fire, which
must soon burst out into a terrible conflagration.

There were a good few Backstagers about. Apparently,
this was one of their rare lulls between productions. The
Critics' Circle for *The Seagull* the next day and then, on
the Wednesday, rehearsals for *The Winter's Tale* would
start. Charles visualized Shakespeare getting the same
perfunctory treatment as Chekhov.

Hugo introduced him liberally to everyone in sight and
then left him to fend for himself. Geoffrey Winter was
lounging against the bar with a middle-aged balding man
dressed in a navy and white striped T-shirt, white
trousers, plimsolls and a silly little blue cap with a gold
anchor on it.

This refugee from *H.M.S. Pinafore* turned out to be
Shad Scott-Smith, director of *The Seagull*. "Now,
Charles," he emoted when they were introduced,
"promise me one thing—that when you do the Critics'
Circle you will really criticize. Treat us just as you would a
professional company. Be cruel if you like, but please,
please, do be constructive. There's an awful tendency for
these meetings to end up just as a sort of mutual
admiration society, which really doesn't help anyone."

"I'll do my best to avoid that."

"Oh, super. I'm just here actually buying the odd drink
of thanks for members of my hardworking cast—
libations to my little gods, you could say. Oh, the whole
gang did work so hard. I tell you, I'm still a washed-out

rag at the end of it all. Still, I at least get a bit of a break now. Do you know, Geoff's going straight on to play Leontes in *The Winter's Tale*. Honestly, I don't know where he gets the energy. How do you do it, Geoff?"

Geoffrey Winter shrugged. Charles thought that was a pretty good answer to a totally fatuous question. He warmed to the man.

Shad went on. "Oh, something happens, I know. The old adrenalin flows. Leave it to Doctor Footlights, he'll sort you out."

He breathed between gushes and changed the subject. "By the way, Geoff, do you know if Charlotte's going to be in this evening? I do want to buy my darling Nina a drink."

"I've no idea what she's up to. Ask Hugo."

Charlotte's husband was hunched over a large Scotch at the bar. Shad swanned over. "Any idea what the little woman's up to this evening?"

"Little woman?" Charles heard a dangerous undertone in Hugo's echo.

"Darling Charlotte," Shad explained.

"Darling Charlotte..." Hugo began, unnecessarily loud. "Darling Charlotte may be in hell for all I know. Don't ask me about Charlotte the harlot. She's a bloody whore!"

After the shocked silence which followed this pronouncement, Shad decided that he'd ring Charlotte from home. As he minced away, other Backstagers joined the exodus with desultory farewells. Charles felt guilty, responsible. "Geoffrey, has Hugo driven them away? He's drunk out of his mind."

"No, it's not that. This place is used to dramatic outbursts. The mass evacuation is due to the telly. *I, Claudius* tonight. Nine o'clock. Becoming a great cult show. I haven't seen any, been rehearsing. But I'm told it's just the thing for bourgeois commuters' wish-fulfilment. Lots of rapes and murders."

"Living vicariously."

"Yes, well, we don't get all that at home. At least, not many of us."

Charles laughed. "Actually, I'd better get Hugo home. I hate to think how much alcohol he's got inside him." He moved over to the bar. "Hugo, time to go, don't you think?"

Once again this suggestion touched some trigger of violence. Hugo shouted, "Just keep your bloody mouth shut!" and dashed his glass of Scotch in Charles' face.

Charles was furious. Unaware of the shocked gaze of the remaining Backstagers, he turned on Hugo. "You're drunk and disgusting!"

"Get lost!"

"You ought to go home. You've had enough."

"I'll go home when I bloody choose to. And that won't be before closing time." Hugo banged his glass down on the bar and then, as if to deny the force of his outburst, asked politely, "May I have another Scotch, please?"

As Robert Chubb obliged with the drink, Charles stormed out. In the lobby he found Geoffrey Winter had followed him. Geoffrey offered a blue and white handkerchief to mop up his jacket. "Thanks. Is there a phone?"

"There. Just behind the door."

Charles got through to Charlotte. "Look, I've just left Hugo. He's in the Backstagers' bar. Says he won't be leaving till it closes. He's extremely drunk."

"Won't be the first time," she said dryly. "Thanks for the warning."

Geoffrey Winter was still waiting outside. "I'd offer you a lift, but we don't run a car. Still, I can show you a quick way down to the station. There's a footpath."

"Thank you."

They walked past a large house next door to the Backstagers. It was neo-Tudor with diamond window panes. No lights on. Outside the porch, horribly out of period, a pair of grotesque stone lions stood on guard.

Charles drew in his breath sharply with distaste.

Geoffrey followed his glance and chuckled. "The Hobbses. Mr. and Mrs. Arkadina. Advertising their money. Ostentatious buggers. But, nonetheless, a good source of free drinks."

Charles laughed, though inwardly he was still seething from the encounter with Hugo.

"By the way," said Geoffrey, "I gather we see you tomorrow."

"Yes, Vee invited me down for a meal. If that's still okay."

"Fine. Love to see you. I'll show you the way when we get to the main road."

They walked across a common where a huge pile of wood and rubbish announced the approach of Bonfire Night.

"Good God, November already," observed Geoffrey. "Guy Fawkes to be burnt again on Friday. How time flies as you get older."

"You think you've got problems," Charles mourned. "It's my fiftieth birthday this week."

They talked a little on the way to the main road, but most of the time there was silence except for the soft pad of their rubber soles on the pathway. Charles didn't notice the lack of conversation. His mind was still full of hurt after the clash with Hugo.

He didn't really notice saying goodbye to Geoffrey. Or the train journey back to Waterloo. He was still seething, almost sick with rage.

Five...

CHARLES SPENT AN unsatisfactory Tuesday mooching round his bedsitter in Hereford Road, Bayswater. It was a depressing room and the fact that he stayed there to do anything but sleep meant he was depressed.

He was still fuming over the scene with Hugo. No longer fuming at the fact that Hugo had hit him, but now angry with himself for having flared up. Hugo was in a really bad state, possibly on the verge of a major breakdown, and, as a friend, Charles should have stood by him, tried to help, not rushed off in a huff after a drunken squabble.

As usual, his dissatisfaction with himself spilled over into other areas of his life. Frances. He must sort out what his relationship with Frances was. They must meet. He must ring her.

Early in the afternoon he went down to the pay-phone on the landing, but before he dialled her number, he realized she wouldn't be there. She was a teacher. Tuesday in term-time she'd be at school. He'd ring her about six, before he went down to Breckton.

To shift his mood, he started looking through his old scripts. *How's Your Father?* He read the first few pages. It really wasn't bad. Light, but fun. A performance by the Backstagers would be better than nothing. Rather sheepishly, he decided to take it with him.

He left without ringing Frances.

Vee Winter opened the door. She had on a P.V.C. apron with a design of an old London omnibus. She looked at him challengingly again, part provocative, part exhibitionist.

"Sorry I'm a bit early, Vee. The train didn't take as long as I expected."

"No, they put on some fast ones during the rush-hour. But don't worry, supper's nearly ready. Geoff's just got in. He's up in the study. Go and join him. He's got some booze up there."

The house was a small Edwardian semi, but it had been rearranged and decorated with taste and skill. Or rather, someone had started rearranging and decorating it with taste and skill. As he climbed the stairs, Charles noticed that the wall had been stripped and rendered, but not yet repapered. In the same way, someone had begun to sand the paint off the banister. Most of the wood was bare, but obstinate streaks of white paint clung in crevices. The house gave the impression that someone had started to renovate it with enormous vigor and then run out of enthusiasm. Or money.

The soprano wailing of the *Liebestod* from Wagner's *Tristan und Isolde* drew him to Geoffrey Winter's study. Here the conversion had very definitely been completed. Presumably the room had been intended originally as a bedroom, but it was now lined with long pine shelves which extended at opposite ends of the room to make a desk and a surface for an impressive selection of hi-fi. The shelves were covered with a cunning disarray of books, models, old bottles and earthenware pots. The predominant color was a pale, pale mustard, which toned in well with the pine. On the wall facing the garden French windows gave out on to a small balcony.

Geoffrey Winter was fiddling with his hi-fi. The Wagner disc was being played on an expensive-looking grey metal turntable. Leads ran from the tuner to a small Japanese cassette radio.

"Sorry, Charles, just getting this on to cassette. So much handier. It's nearly finished."

"This room's really good, Geoffrey."

"I like it. One of the advantages of not having children—you have space."

"And more money."

Geoffrey grimaced. "Hmm. Depends on the size of your mortgage. And your other bills. And how work's going."

"What do you do?"

"I'm an architect." Which explained the skill of the decor.

"Work for yourself?"

"Yes. Well, that is to say, I work for whoever will pay for my services. So at the moment, yes, I seem to work just for myself. No one's building anything. Can I get you a drink?"

"Thank you."

"It's sherry or sherry, I'm afraid." And, Charles noticed, not a particularly good sherry. Cypress domestic. Tut, tut, getting spoiled by the ostentatious array of Hugo's drinks cupboard. It would take a distressingly short time to pick up all the little snobberies of materialism.

While Geoffrey poured the drinks, Charles moved over to the shelves to inspect a theatrical model he had noticed when he came in. It was a stage set of uneven levels and effectively placed columns. Plastic figures were grouped on the rostra.

Geoffrey answered the unspoken question as he handed Charles his sherry. "Set for *The Caucasian Chalk Circle*. I'm directing it for the Backstagers in the new year."

"You're a meticulous planner."

"I think as a director you have to be. In anything to do with the theatre, in fact. You have to have planned every detail."

"Yes, I could tell that from your Trigorin."

"I'm not sure whether that's meant to be a compliment or not, Charles."

"Nor am I."

Geoffrey laughed.

"No, Geoffrey, what I mean is, you had more stagecraft than the rest of the company put together, but occasionally...one or two tricks—like that very slow delivery on key lines, separating the words, giving each equal emphasis—well, I was conscious of the artifice."

Geoffrey smiled, perhaps with slight restraint. "Don't waste it, Charles. Keep it for the Critics' Circle. Professional criticism."

The record had ended. The stylus worried against the center groove. Geoffrey seemed suddenly aware of it and, with a look at Charles, he switched off the cassette player. He replaced the disc in its sleeve and marshalled it into a rack.

The conversation dipped. Charles found himself asking about the previous night's television. Dear, oh dear. Slipping into commuter habits. "Did you get back in time for your ration of rape and murder in *I, Claudius* last night?"

"No. I was back in time, but I left Vee to watch it on her own. I did some work on Leontes. Trying to learn the bloody lines."

"Shakespearean verse at its most tortured. How do you learn them? Have you any magic method?"

"'Fraid not. It's just read through, read through. Time and again."

"It's the only way."

At that moment Vee called from downstairs to say the meal was ready.

There was quite a crowd in the Back Room before the Critics' Circle. And for once they had a topic of conversation other than the theatrical doings of the Breckton Backstagers.

Denis and Mary Hobbs had been burgled. They had come home from their weekend cottage at about midnight the previous night and found the house full of police. A burglar had smashed one of the diamond panes in a downstairs front window, reached through and opened it, gone upstairs and emptied the contents of Mary's jewel box.

". . . That's what's so horrible about it," she was saying into her fourth consolatory double gin, " the idea of someone in your house, going through your things. It's ghastly."

"Were they vandals too? Did they dirty your bedclothes and scrawl obscenities on your walls?" asked sour Reggie hopefully.

"No, at least we were spared that. Remarkably tidy burglars, closed all the cupboards and doors after them. No fingerprints either, so the C.I.D. boys tell us. But . . ." After her proprietory reference to the police force, she warmed to her role as tragic queen. ". . . that only seems to make it worse. It was so coldblooded. And the idea of other people invading our privacy—ooh, it makes me feel cold all over."

"Did they get much?" asked Reggie, with morbid interest.

"Oh yes, there was quite a lot of good stuff in my jewellery box. Not everyday things—I dare say a lot of them I don't wear more than twice a year. But I'd got them out of the bank for this Masonic do of Denis's last Monday and it didn't seem worth putting them back, because next week there's this dinner-dance thing at the Hilton—did I tell you about that?"

The snide expressions on the faces of the surrounding Backstagers suggested that Mary missed no opportunity to give them details of her posh social life. Anyway, the question seemed to be rhetorical. The role was shifting from tragic queen to wonderful person.

"Oh, I don't care about the stuff as jewellery. I'm not

materialistic. But they're presents Den's given me over the years, birthdays, Christmases and so on. That's the trouble—the insurance will cover the value in money terms, but it can never replace what those things mean to me."

"It serves us bloody right," said her husband. "We've talked enough times about having a burglar alarm put in. But you put it off. You think it'll never happen to you."

"Do the police reckon there's a chance of getting the culprits?"

"I don't know. Never commit themselves, the buggers, do they? But I think it's unlikely. They seem to reckon the best chance was missed when Bob first saw the light."

"What light?"

"Oh, didn't you hear? You tell them, Bob."

Robert Chubb took his cue and graciously moved to center stage. "I was the one who discovered the ghastly crime. Proper little Sherlock Holmes. Perhaps I should take it up professionally.

"I'd been sorting through some stuff in the office last night after I handed the bar over to Reggie and I was walking home past Denis and Mary's at about ten-fifteen, when I saw this light."

Years of amateur dramatics would not allow him to miss the pregnant pause. "The light was just by the broken window. It shone on the jagged glass. I thought immediately of burglars and went back to the office to phone the police. Incidentally—" he added in self-justification, in case Denis's last remark might be construed by anyone as a criticism, "the boys in blue told me I was absolutely right not to try to tackle the criminal. Said they get as much trouble from members of the public who fancy themselves as heroes as they do from the actual crooks.

"Anyway, my intervention does not seem to have been completely useless. They reckon the burglar must have seen me and that's what frightened him off. He appears to have scampered away in some disarray."

"Yes," Mary Hobbs chipped in, temperamentally

unsuited to listening to anyone for that length of time.
"He left his torch behind in the window sill. The police are
hoping to be able to trace him through that."

Robert Chubb, piqued at losing his punch-line,
changed the subject. Like a child who dictates the rules of
the game because it's his ball, he brought them back to his
dramatic society. "Oh, Charles, about the World
Premières Festival, did you bring along that play of
yours? The committee would really like to have a look at
it. Need a good new play, you know."

Embarrassed at the fact that he actually had got it with
him, Charles handed over the script with some apology
about it being very light.

"Oh, the lighter the better. I'm sure it has the
professional touch. And, talking of that, I do hope that in
your criticism this evening you will apply professional
standards to *The Seagull*. We always do and hope others
will. So please don't pull your punches."

"All right. I won't."

As soon as Charles started speaking to the rows of earnest
Backstagers in the rehearsal room, it was clear that they
did not like being judged by professional standards.

He began with a few general observations on Chekhov
and the difficulties that his plays presented. He referred to
the years of work which had gone into the Moscow Arts
Theatre's productions. He then went into detail on
Chekhovian humor and stressed the inadvisability of
playing Russian servants as mugging Mummerset yokels.

He moved on from this to the rest of the cast. He gave a
general commendation and then made detailed criticism.
He praised Charlotte's controlled innocence as Nina and
the technical skill of Geoffrey's Trigorian. He faulted
Clive Steele's Konstantin for lack of discipline and
regretted that the part of Madame Arkadina was beyond
the range of all but a handful of the world's actresses. But,
rather against his better judgement and to sugar the pill,
he congratulated Mary Hobbs on a brave attempt.

He thought he had been fair. Out of deference to their

amateur status and because he had no desire to cause unpleasantness, he had toned down the criticism he would have given a professional cast. He thought his remarks might have been overindulgent, but otherwise unexceptionable.

The shocked silence which followed his conclusion indicated that the Backstagers did not share his opinion. Reggie, who seemed to get lumbered with (or perhaps sought after) all official functions, was chairing the meeting. He rose to his feet. "Well, some fairly controversial views there from Mr. Parrish. I don't think everyone's going to agree with all that." A murmur of agreement came back from the audience. "Still, thank you. Any questions?"

There was an "after you" silence and then Shad Scott-Smith rose to his feet. He spoke with a heavy irony which obviously appealed to the mood of the gathering. "Well, first of all, I'd like to thank Mr. Parrish for his comments and what I'd like to offer is not so much a question as a humble defence.

"As perpetrator of the terrible crime of *The Seagull...*" This sally drew an appreciative titter. "I feel I should apologize, both to the cast, whom I misled so disastrously, and to the good folk of Breckton, who so unwisely bought all the tickets for all four performances and who made the terrible mistake of enjoying the production very much."

This got an outright laugh of self-congratulation. "And I would also like to apologize to the local newspaper critics who, out of sheer malice and stupidity, gave such good reviews to my production of *The Cherry Orchard* last year, since they didn't know they were dealing with someone who had no appreciation of Chekhov. And while I'm at it, I'd better tick off the adjudicators of the Inter-Regional Drama Festival who were foolish enough to award my production of *The Bear* a Special Commendation."

He sat down to a riot of applause. Charles saw he was going to have an uphill fight. "All right, I'm sorry. I had no intention of offending anyone. I am here as a professional actor and director and I'm giving you my opinions as I would to the members of a professional company. Everyone keeps saying that these Critics' Circles are not just meant to be a mutual admiration society."

"No, they're certainly not," said Robert Chubb with unctuous charm. "I set them up as a forum for informed discussion, for the give-and-take of intelligent ideas. I'm sure we can all take criticism and that's what we are all here for."

Charles thought maybe at last he had got a supporter. But Robert Chubb soon dispelled the idea as he went on. "The only comment I would have is that it does seem to me rather a pity that the only member of the cast for whom you managed unstinting praise was one of our newest members and that you were somewhat dismissive of some of our most experienced actors and actresses. Particularly of a lady to whom we all owe many splendid performances, not least her Lady Macbeth last year."

This spirited defence of Mary Hobbs produced another warm burst of applause. Charles was tempted to ask what relevance a performance in a production of *Macbeth* he couldn't possibly have seen should have to a production of *The Seagull* he had seen, but there didn't seem any point.

He had misjudged the nature of the meeting entirely. All that had been required of him had been a pat on the back for all concerned, not forgetting the charming young man who tore his ticket and the good ladies who made the coffee for the interval. All he could do now was to insure that that meeting ended as soon as possible and get the hell out of the place. And never come back.

Mentally he cursed Hugo for ever letting him in for it, or at least for not briefing him as to what to expect.

He then realized with a slight shock that Hugo wasn't there. Nor was Charlotte. Nor Clive Steele. It seemed strange.

As he thought about it, he started again to feel guilty

about the way he had left Hugo the night before. He hated to let things like that fester. Stupid misunderstandings should be cleared up as soon as possible. He was too old to lose friends over trivialities. Once he'd stopped the Backstagers baying for his blood, he'd go round and see Hugo and apologize.

But there was still more Critics' Circling to be weathered. It was hard work. There was no common ground for discussion. The Backstagers were only capable of talking about the Backstagers. When Charles made a comparison with a West End production of *The Three Sisters*, someone would say, "Well, of course, when Walter directed it down here..." When he praised the comic timing of Michael Hordern, someone would say, "Oh, but Philip's a wonderful actor too. If you'd seen him in *The Rivals*..." It was like talking to a roomful of politicians. Every question was greeted, not by an answer, but by an aggrieved assertion of something totally different.

It did end. Eventually. Reggie gave an insipid vote of thanks with some vague remarks about "having been given lots of food for thought...interesting, and even surprising, to hear the views of someone from the outside."

Charles prepared his getaway. He thanked Geoffrey and Vee for the meal and made for the exit, hoping that he was seeing the last of the Breckton Backstagers.

As he reached the door, he overheard a lacquered voice commenting, "Don't know who he thinks he is anyway. I've never seen him on the television or anything."

Charles Paris knew who they were talking about.

Hugo opened the front door. His eyes were dull and registered no surprise at the visit. He was still wearing the clothes he had had on the day before and their scruffy appearance suggested he hadn't been to bed in the interim. The smell of whisky which blasted from him suggested that he hadn't stopped drinking either.

"I came round to apologize for going off like that last night."

"Apologize," Hugo echoed stupidly. He didn't seem to know what Charles was talking about.

"Yes. Can I come in?"

"Sure. Have a drink." Hugo led the way, stumbling, into the sitting room. It was a mess. Empty whisky bottles of various brands bore witness to a long session. He must have been working through the collection. Incongruously, the scene was cosily lit by an open fire, heaped with glowing smokeless fuel.

"Was cold," Hugo mumbled by way of explanation. He swayed towards the fire and removed the still burning gas poker. "Shouldn't have left that in." He unscrewed the lead with excessive concentration. "Whisky?"

"Thank you."

Hugo slopped out half a tumbler of Glenlivet and handed it over. "Cheers." He slumped into an armchair with his own glass.

Charles took a long sip. It was welcome after the idiocies of the Critics' Circle. "Where's Charlotte?"

"Huh. Charlotte." Hugo spoke without violence, but with great bitterness. "Charlotte's finished."

"What do you mean?"

"Charlotte—finished. The great love affair, Charlotte and Hugo—over."

"You mean she's left you?"

"Not here." Hugo was almost incoherent.

"She wasn't here when you got back last night?"

"Not here."

"Where do you think she's gone?"

"I don't know. To see lover boy."

"Is there a lover boy?"

"I suppose so. That's the usual story. Pretty young girl. Middle-aged husband. Don't you read the Sunday papers?" Hugo spoke in a low, hopeless mumble.

"Have you been in to work today?" Hugo shook his head. "Just drinking?" A small nod.

They sat and drank. Charles tried to think of anything he could say that might be helpful. There was nothing. He could only stay, be there.

After a long, long silence, he started to feel cold. The fire was nearly dead. Charles got up briskly. "Where's the coal, Hugo? I'll go and get some more."

"You'll never find it. Let me. Come on, I'll show you."

Hugo led the way unsteadily into the kitchen. He picked up a torch and fumbled it on.

They went out of the back door. There was a shed just opposite. "In there," said Hugo.

Charles opened the door. Hugo shone the torch.

In its beam they saw Charlotte. She was splayed unceremoniously over the coal. A scarf was knotted unnaturally round her neck. She was very dead.

Six...

CHARLES RANG THE police and stayed beside Hugo
in the sitting room until they arrived. Hugo was catatonic
with shock. Only once did he speak, murmuring softly to
himself, "What did I do to her? She was young. What did I
do to her?"

When the police arrived, Charles steeled himself to go
out once again to the coal shed. The beams of their
torches were stronger and made the color of Charlotte's
cheeks even less natural, like a detail from an over-
exposed photograph.

The richness of her perfume, which still hung in the air,
was sickly and inappropriate. The staring eyes and untidy
spread of limbs were not horrifying; the feeling they gave
Charles was more one of embarrassment, as if a young girl
had been sick at a party. And his impression of callowness
was reinforced by the Indian print scarf over the bruised
neck, like a teenager's attempt to hide love-bites.

The bruises were chocolate brown. On one of them the

skin had been broken and a bootlace of dried blood traced its way crazily up towards Charlotte's mouth.

Hugo remained dull and silent and Charles himself was dazed as they were driven to the police station. They were separated when they arrived and parted without a word. Each was taken into a separate interview room to make a statement.

Charles had to wait for about half an hour before his questioning began. A uniformed constable brought him a cup of tea and apologized for the delay. Everyone was very pleasant, but pleasant with that slight restraint that staff have in hospitals, as if something unpleasant is happening nearby but no one is going to mention it.

Eventually two policemen came in. One was in uniform and carried a sheaf of paper. The other was fair-haired, early thirties, dressed in a brown blazer and blue trousers. He spoke with the vestiges of a South London twang. "So sorry to have kept you waiting. Detective-Sergeant Harvey. Mr. Paris, isn't it?"

Charles nodded.

"Fine. I must just get a few personal details and then, if I may, I'll ask a few questions about . . . what happened. Then Constable Renton will write it down as a statement, which you sign—if you're happy with it. Okay?"

Charles nodded again.

"It's late, and I'm afraid this could take some time. Say if you'd like more tea. Or a sandwich or something."

"No, I'm fine, thanks."

So it started. First, simple information, name, address and so on. Then details of how he came to know Mr. and Mrs. Mecken. And then a resume of the last two days.

As he spoke, Charles could feel it going wrong. He told the truth, he told it without bias, and yet he could feel the false picture that his words were building up. Everything he said seemed to incriminate Hugo. The more he tried to defend him, the worse it sounded.

Detective-Sergeant Harvey was a good poker-faced

questioner. He didn't force the pace, he didn't put words into Charles's mouth, he just asked for information slowly and unemotionally. And to damning effect.

"After your lunch on Monday you say that you and Mr. Mecken went on to a drinking club?"

"Yes, a sort of strip joint in Dean Street."

"And what did you drink there?"

"Hugo ordered a bottle of whisky."

"So, by the time you left there, you had both had a considerable amount to drink?"

"I didn't drink a great deal in the club." Immediately Charles kicked himself for prompting the next question.

"But Mr. Mecken did?"

"I suppose he had quite a bit by some people's standards, but you know how it is with advertising people—they can just drink and drink." The attempt at humor didn't help. It made it sound more and more of a whitewash.

"Yes. But you then both returned to Breckton and continued drinking at the theatre club. Surely that made it rather a lot of alcohol, even for an advertising man."

"Well, yes, I agree, we wouldn't normally have drunk that much, but you see Hugo was a bit upset and..." Realizing that once again he had said exactly the wrong thing, Charles left the words hanging in the air.

"Upset," Detective-Sergeant Harvey repeated without excitement. "Have you any idea why he should have been upset?"

Charles hedged. "Oh, I dare say it was something at work. He was involved in a big campaign to launch a new bedtime drink—that's what I was working on with him—and I think there may have been some disagreements over that. You know, these advertising people do take it all so seriously."

"Yes. Of course." The slow response seemed only to highlight the hollowness of Charles's words. "You have no reason to believe that Mr. Mecken was having any domestic troubles?"

"Domestic troubles?" Charles repeated idiotically.

"Worries about his marriage."

"Oh. Oh, I shouldn't think so. I mean, I don't know. I don't think anyone can begin to understand anything about another person's marriage. But I mean Charlotte is a—I mean, was a beautiful girl and..." He trailed off guiltily.

"Hmm. Mr. Paris, would you describe Mr. Mecken as a violent man?"

"No, certainly not. And if you're trying to suggest that—"

"I am not trying to suggest anything, Mr. Paris. I am just trying to get as full a background to the death of Mrs. Mecken as I can," Detective-Sergeant Harvey replied evenly.

"Yes, of course, I'm sorry." Blustering wasn't going to help Hugo's cause. As his interrogation continued, Charles kept thinking of his friend, in another interview room, being asked other questions. Where were Hugo's answers leading?

"You say Mr. Mecken is not a habitually violent man. Is he perhaps the sort who might become violent when he's had a few drinks? I mean, for instance, did he show any violence towards you during your long drinking session on Monday?"

Charles hesitated. Certainly he wasn't going to go back to Hugo's bizarre outbursts while an undergraduate and his instinct was to deny that anything had happened on the Monday. But Hugo's second swing at him had been witnessed by a bar full of Backstagers. He couldn't somehow see that self-dramatizing lot keeping quiet about it. He'd do better to edit the truth than to tell a lie. "Well, he did take a sort of playful swing at me at one point when I suggested he ought to be getting home, but that's all."

"A playful swing." Detective-Sergeant Harvey gave the three words equal emphasis.

The questioning ended soon after and the information

was turned into a written statement. Detective-Sergeant Harvey courteously went through a selection of the questions again and Constable Renton laboriously wrote down the answers in longhand on ruled paper.

Inevitably it was a slow process and Charles found his mind wandering. He didn't like the way it was heading.

Previously he had been numb with shock, but now the fact of Charlotte's death was getting through to him. The feeling of guilt which his initially casual reaction had prompted gave way to a cold sensation of nausea.

With it came a realization of the implications for Hugo. As Charles went through the details for his statement, he saw with horror which way the circumstantial evidence pointed.

There were so many witnesses too. So many people who had heard Hugo's denunciation of his wife and his violent burst of aggression towards Charles. Unless Hugo could prove a very solid alibi for the time at which his wife had been murdered, things didn't look too good for him.

At this point it struck Charles that he was assuming Hugo was innocent and he paused to question the logic of this. On reflection, it didn't stand up very well. In fact the only arguments he could come up with against Hugo's guilt were Hugo's own denial that he would ever hurt Charlotte and Charles's own conviction that someone he knew so well would be incapable of a crime of such savagery.

And those weren't arguments. They were sheer emotion, romantic indulgence.

The thought of romanticism only made it worse. It suggested a very plausible motive for Hugo to kill his wife. Hugo was a romantic, unwilling to accept the unpleasant facts of life. He had built up his own life into a romantic ideal, with his writing talent supporting the professional side and his love-affair with Charlotte the domestic.

When it became clear to such a man that the twin pillars of his life were both illusions, anything could happen.

He finished the statement and was asked to read it through, signing each page. At one point he hesitated.

"Anything wrong?" asked Detective-Sergeant Harvey.

"Well, I . . . it seems so bald, so . . ." He couldn't think of anything that didn't sound like protesting too much. "No." He signed on.

He was amazed to discover it was nearly five o'clock. Dully he accepted the offer of the lift home in a squad car. He gave his Hereford Road address.

He didn't notice the drabness of the bedsitter as he entered. He homed in on the bottle of Bells straight away and sank half a tumblerful. Then he lay down on the bed and lost consciousness.

When he woke, it was still dark. Or rather, he realized after looking at his watch, dark again. Quarter past six. He'd slept round the clock.

He was still dressed. He left the house and walked along Hereford Road to Westbourne Grove. There was a newspaper seller on the corner. He bought an *Evening Standard*.

It didn't take long to find the news. Hugo Mecken had been arrested, charged with the murder of his wife, Charlotte.

And Charles Paris felt it was his fault.

Seven...

IN SPITE OF logic, the feeling of treachery remained. Charles Paris had deserted his friend in a crisis. Charles Paris had incriminated his friend by his statement.

He had to do something. At least find out all the circumstances, at least check that no mistakes had been made.

He hurried back to the house in Hereford Road, went to the pay-phone on the landing and dialled Gerald Venables's office number.

Gerald was a successful show business solicitor whom Charles had known since Oxford. Armed with a boyish enthusiasm for the whole business of detection, he had collaborated with Charles on one or two investigations, starting with the strange death of Marius Steen. In the current circumstances, it was an immediate instinct to ring Gerald.

An efficient, husky voice answered the phone.

"Is that Polly?"

"Yes."

"It's Charles Paris. Could I speak to Gerald, please?"

"I'm sorry, he's not here."

"Oh, sod it. Is he on his way home?"

"No, he's out with a client, I'm afraid. He was called down to Breckton mid-morning and he's been there all day."

"Oh my God, of course. He's Hugo Mecken's solicitor, isn't he?"

"Yes. That's who he's with. I gather you've heard the news."

"Yes." It wasn't worth going into details of how he had been the first to hear it. "Stupid of me. I'd forgotten. Gerald sorted out Hugo's divorce, didn't he?"

"Yes. And he was a bit shocked when he discovered what it was about this time."

"That I can believe. Look, Polly, have you any idea when he'll be back? I mean, is he reckoning to go back to the office?"

"No. He rang about half an hour ago to say he'd go straight to Dulwich from Breckton. And asked me to ring Mrs. Venables and say he'd be late."

"Why didn't he ring her himself?" Charles asked irrelevantly.

"I think it sounds more businesslike if I do," Polly replied with a hint of humor.

Yes, that was Gerald all over. "Polly, when he says 'very late,' what do you reckon that means?"

"I honestly don't know. He said I was to say ten-thirty at the earliest to Mrs. Venables."

"Okay. Thanks, Polly. He didn't say anything else about . . . you know, the case . . . or Hugo . . . or anything."

"No. Well, there isn't really much to say, is there?"

"I suppose not."

Charles spent an unsatisfactory evening and drank too much. He thought of ringing Frances, but put it off again. Round eight he realized he hadn't eaten for over twenty-four hours. He didn't feel hungry, but he thought he ought to have something.

Going out to a restaurant was too much effort. He was too jumpy to sit down and relax over a proper meal. He looked round the room. There was an opened packet of cornflakes on the table. No milk. He tried a handful. They were soft, cardboard.

He rooted through the grey-painted cupboard, shoving aside scripts, half-finished plays, empty bottles, socks and crisp packets. All he came up with was a tin of sardines without a key and a tin of curried beans.

The menu was dictated by his antiquated tin-opener, which wouldn't grip on the sardine tin. He slopped the beans into a saucepan still furred with boiled milk from the previous week and put it on the gas-ring which was hidden discreetly behind a plastic curtain.

The curried beans didn't improve anything. He took a long swill from the Bell's bottle as a mouthwash. Except he didn't spit it out.

Then he addressed his mind to thought. Serious thought. He had been in criminal situations before and he had even, by a mixture of luck and serendipity, solved crimes before. But this one mattered. He had to concentrate, sort it out. He was motivated by his affection for Hugo and his abiding sense of guilt.

His first assumption remained Hugo's innocence. No logic for this, just a conviction.

If only he could see Hugo face to face, talk to him, ask him, Then he would know, he felt sure.

But how do you get to see a man who has just been arrested for murder? Gerald would know. All action seemed to hinge on speaking to Gerald.

Half past nine. The evening was passing, but slowly. Perhaps another generous Bell's would speed up the process.

He looked at the floor through the slopping spirit in his glass. The image was refracted and distorted. Like his thought processes.

The obvious solution was that Hugo had killed his wife. In a wild reaction to the collapse of his dreams he had taken the terrible kamikaze course of the disillusioned romantic. "Yet each man kills the thing he loves...," as Oscar Wilde wrote in his despair.

The only way to escape the obvious solution was to provide a feasible alternative. Either to prove Hugo was doing something else at the time that Charlotte was killed. Or to prove that someone else did it.

Charles's brief experience of the Backstagers told him that emotions ran high in the group. Charlotte had antagonized the established stars by her success as Nina. Vee Winter, for one, felt herself usurped by the newcomer.

But that kind of jealousy wasn't sufficient motive for murder. A sexual impulse was more likely. A woman as beautiful as Charlotte was bound to cause reverberations wherever she went and no doubt her appearance among the Backstagers had led to the snapping-off of a few middle-aged husbands' heads by middle-aged wives who saw eyes lingering with too much interest. Indeed, Charles had seen evidence of this with the Hobbses.

But that was still not something for which a sane person would kill.

It must be a closer attachment. Clive Steele. Charles thought back over the conversation he had heard in the car park. The young man's passions had been demonstrably immature, but they had been strong. He was supposed to be away working in Melton Mowbray for the whole week, but it might be worth investigating his movements.

Or then again, why should the murderer have anything to do with the Backstagers? Charlotte did have other contacts. Not many but a few. Diccon Hudson, for instance. He had made some sour reference to having gone around with her before her marriage. Probably nothing there, but anything was worth looking into to save Hugo.

After all, Diccon could have been the mysterious lover of whom Hugo had spoken. Charles didn't know whether to believe in this personage or not. It could just be a creation of Hugo's fevered imagination. But if such a person did exist, the possible permutations of violent emotions were considerably increased.

Equally, if he did exist, Hugo's motive for killing his wife was that much stronger. But Charles put the thought from his mind. He had to start by assuming Hugo's innocence.

He was full of nervous excitement. He wanted to do something, get started, begin his task of atonement.

He looked at his watch. Twenty-five to eleven. Thank God, he could try Gerald again. The need to do something was now almost unbearable.

Kate, Gerald's wife, sounded disgruntled. No, he wasn't home yet. Yes, Charles could try again in half an hour if it was important, but not much later because she was going to bed.

Charles stood by the phone, seething with energy There must be something else he could do. He could start piecing together Hugo's movements from the time he left the Back Room on the Monday night. Someone must have seen him leave, someone might even have walked him home. Details like that could be vital.

The only Backstager's number he had was Geoffrey and Vee's. Geoffrey answered.

"Have you heard about Hugo?"

"Yes, Charles. Horrible, isn't it?"

"Horrible. Look, I'm trying to find out what he did when he left the bar on Monday night."

"Amateur sleuth work."

"I don't know. Maybe. Thing is, you'd know—who are the real barflies up at that place? Who was guaranteed to have been there at closing time and seen him go?"

"Well, Bob Chubb's the obvious one. He was on the bar, wasn't he?"

"Do you have his number?"

"Yes, sure. I'll get it. I—what's that, love?" Vee's voice was asking something in the background. "Just twiddle the aerial round to the right. Sorry, Charles, our television's on the blink. Extremely unwilling to get a decent picture on BBC2. Comes of buying cheap junk. Ah, here it is." He gave Charles Robert Chubb's number. "I only hope it bears fruit. It seems incredible, doesn't it? The idea that Hugo ... I keep thinking that it'll all turn out to be a mistake and all be cleared up somehow."

"It depends what you mean by cleared up. Charlotte will still be dead."

"Yes."

Robert Chubb answered the phone. His voice was bland and elocuted. When it heard who was calling, it took on a colder note. And when it heard what Charles wanted to know, it became positively snappish.

"As I have already told the police, Mr. Mecken left the bar at about ten-thirty. On his own. I don't really know why I should waste my time repeating this to you. I know everyone likes to see themselves as a private eye, but I really do suggest, Mr. Parrish, that you should leave criminal investigation to the professionals."

"And I really do suggest, Mr. Chubb, that you should do the same with the theatre." Charles slammed the phone down.

He was beginning to run out of small change. He rested his penultimate 10p on the slot and dialled Gerald's number again.

The solicitor answered, sounding formal, even pettish. "Oh, hello, Charles, Kate said you'd rung. Look, could you ring me later on tomorrow? I'm dog-tired. I've just got in and I'm sure whatever you've got to say will keep."

"Gerald, it's about Hugo."

"Oh. Oh yes, of course, you were with him when he found the body—or claimed to find it."

"Yes. How's it going?"

"What do you mean—how's it going?"

"With Hugo."

"Charles, I'm sorry." Gerald sounded exasperated and professional. "I know you are a friend and we are talking about a mutual friend, but I'm afraid, as a solicitor, I can't discuss my clients' affairs."

"You can tell me where he is, can't you? Is he in prison—or where?"

"He'll be spending tonight in the cells at Breckton Police Station."

"And then what?"

Gerald sighed with annoyance. "Tomorrow morning he'll appear at Breckton Magistrates' Court where he'll be remanded in custody. Which means Brixton. Then he'll be remanded again every week until the trial."

"Hmm. When can I get to see him?"

"See him—what do you mean?"

"You know, see him. I want to ask him some questions."

"Well, I don't know. I suppose it may be possible for him to have visitors when he's in Brixton. I'm not sure how soon—"

"No, I want to see him tomorrow."

"That's impossible."

"Will you be seeing him?"

"Yes, of course. As his solicitor, I'll be in court and see him before he's taken off to Brixton."

"Well, can't I come along with you and be passed off as one of your outfit?"

"One of my *outfit*?" Gerald italicized the last word with distaste.

"Yes, surely you have colleagues in your office, articled clerks and what have you. Pretend I'm one of them."

"Charles, do you realize what you're saying? You are asking me to indulge in serious professional misconduct. Have you been drinking?"

"Yes, of course I have. But that's not the point. I am completely serious."

"Charles, I am also serious. This is an extremely serious matter. We are talking about a case of murder."

"What about the death of Willy Mariello? Wasn't that a case of murder? You were keen enough to help me on that. Indeed, whenever I meet you, you get all schoolboyish and ask me when I'm going to get involved in another case and beg that I'll let you know and work together with you on it."

"Yes, but that's different."

"No, it isn't. The only difference is that this case happens to be one in which you are already involved professionally. So far as I'm concerned, this is a case of murder which might well need investigation and, according to your frequently expressed desire, I am asking you if you will help me on it."

Gerald was silent for a moment. When he spoke again, it was with less certitude. "But, Charles, this is a fairly open-and-shut case. I mean, I know I shouldn't say this about a client, but it seems to me that there's little doubt Hugo did it. It all fits in too neatly. And anyway the police wouldn't have arrested and charged him so quickly if it hadn't been pretty definite."

"Okay, I agree. It is most likely that Hugo murdered Charlotte. But I feel that so long as there's even the vaguest alternative possibility, we should investigate it. Well, I should, anyway. Just for my peace of mind."

"What do you mean by an alternative possibility: '

"Say an alibi. Suppose Hugo saw someone, talked to someone during that missing twenty-four hours...."

"But if he did, surely he would have told the police."

"Yes, probably. Look, I haven't worked it all out yet, but I feel guilty about it and—"

Gerald was continuing his own train of thought. "Anyway, we are only talking of a fairly short period for which he'd need an alibi. The preliminary medical report came in while I was down at the Breckton Police Station. They'll get the full post mortem results in a couple of days. It seems that when you discovered Charlotte's body, she'd already been dead for twenty-four hours."

"Good God. So she was killed on the Monday night."

"Yes. The police theory is that Hugo arrived back from the theatre club smashed out of his mind, had an argument with his wife—possibly over sexual matters—and then ... well, strangled her and hid the body. It fits. He'd had a hell of a lot to drink."

"I see. And I suppose the theory is that he continued drinking through the Tuesday to get over the shock."

"Something like that, yes."

"Hmm. This makes it even more imperative that I see Hugo."

"Charles, I have a professional reputation to—"

"Oh, stuff that, Gerald. For God's sake. You're always complaining to me how bloody boring your work is, how sick you get of fiddling about with theatrical contracts all day, how you wish you could get involved in something really exciting like a murder. Well, here's one right in your in-tray...."

"Yes, and it's just because it's there that I have to treat it with professional propriety."

"Gerald, stop being so bloody pompous. I've got to see Hugo. Look, there's hardly any risk involved. Okay, so you've got a new Mr. Paris on your staff. No one knows you down in Breckton. No one's going to check."

"Well ...," wavering.

Press home advantage. "Come on, Gerald. Live a little. Take a risk. Being a solicitor is the business of seeing how far laws can bend—why not test this one out?"

"I'm not sure."

"Look, you're nearly fifty, Gerald. I don't believe you've ever taken a risk in your life. Even the shows you put money into are all box office certainties. Just try this. Come on, I'll be the one who gets clobbered if anything goes wrong. But nothing will, anyway. Go on, what do you say?"

"Well ... Look, if I do agree, and if you do find out there's anything to be investigated, you will keep me in the picture, won't you?"

"Of course."

There was a long pause. The pay-tone on the phone beeped insistently. Charles crammed in his last 10p. By the time the line was clear, Gerald had reached his decision.

"Okay, buster. We give it a whirl, huh?"

It was going to be all right. When Gerald started talking like a fifties thriller, he was getting interested in a case.

"But one thing, Charles. . . ."

"Yes."

"People who work in my office tend to look extremely smart and well-groomed. So will you see to it that you are wearing a suit, that you've shaved and that you've brushed your hair? I don't want you rolling up in your usual guise of an out-of-work gamekeeper who's just spent a long night with Lady Chatterley."

"Don't worry, Gerald. I'll look as smooth as you do."

Eight ...

GERALD WAS GRUDGING. "Well, I suppose it'll do."

"What do you mean—do?" Charles was aggrieved. He had spent the journey down to Breckton in vivid fantasies of Charles Paris, the legal whiz-kid. As an actor, he could never escape being dictated to by his costumes.

"Never mind. I suppose there are scruffy solicitors," Gerald conceded.

"Scruffy? I'll have you know, in 1965, this suit was considered daringly trendy."

"Yes, maybe, but one or two things have changed since 1965. In fact, most things have."

"Except the British legal system, which hasn't changed since 1865."

Gerald ignored the gibe. He looked preoccupied. "Charles, I've been thinking about this business. As a solicitor, I will be taking a risk which is really unjustifiable. In the sense—"

"It's decided. I've got to see Hugo."

"You'll have to give your name when we enter the

71

court. If there ever is any follow-up—"

"Let's assume there isn't. Come on, Gerald, where's your spirit of adventure?"

"Currently hiding behind my fear of being struck off for professional misconduct."

They entered the Magistrates' Court building. Mr. Venables and his colleague from the office, Mr. Paris, checked in and were directed to the relevant court. They sidled on to a solicitors' bench on which the profession was represented by every level of sartorial elegance.

"That suit on the end's a darned sight older than mine," Charles hissed. "Looks like it escaped from a Chicago gangster movie."

Gerald switched him off with a look. Charles scanned the courtroom. It all seemed a bit lethargic, like a rehearsal where some of the principal actors were missing and their lines were being read in. The court was as empty as a summer matinée. And as in a theatre, where the audience is scattered in little groups, he was more conscious of the comings and goings in his immediate vicinity than of the main action taking place between the magistrates' dais and the dock. Solicitors shuffled in and out, reading long sheets of paper to themselves in states of bored abstraction.

One disturbing feature of the proceedings, for which his ignorance of the British legal system had not prepared him, was the large number of policemen around. That in itself was not worrying, but it soon became apparent that for each case the arresting officer had to be present. He wasn't sure who the arresting officer would be in Hugo's case, but if it were one of the policemen he had met on the Tuesday night, Charles's imposture could have serious consequences. He decided not to mention this new anxiety to Gerald. It would only upset him.

It was after twelve, and after some dreary cases of drunkenness, thefts and a taking and driving away, that Hugo was called. He came up into the dock accompanied by a policeman whom, thank God, Charles had never seen before. The prisoner was not handcuffed; in spite of the seriousness of the charge, he was not regarded as a public danger.

Charles turned round with some trepidation and discovered to his relief that there were no familiar faces among the policemen who had just entered the court.

He transferred his attention to his friend. Hugo looked lifeless. There was a greyish sheen to his face and bald dome; his eyes were dead like pumice-stone. Charles recognised that extinguished expression. He'd seen it in Oxford tutorials, in recording studios, at the various ports of call during their Monday drinking session. Hugo had retreated into his mind, closing the door behind him. Nobody could share what he found there, no friend, no wife.

This time the deadness seemed total, as if Hugo had withdrawn completely from the body. His movements when brought to the dock had been those of an automaton. Presumably he must still be suffering from a brain-crushing hangover—it would take a week or so to get over the sort of bender he had been on—but that wasn't sufficient to explain the absolute impassivity of his expression. It was as if he had opted out of life completely.

The proceedings were short. The charge was read by the magistrate, the police said that they were not yet ready to proceed and the accused was remanded in custody for a week.

Suddenly Hugo was being led off down to the cells again. Gerald shook Charles by the shoulder. "Come on. We go down now."

The jailer was in a lenient mood and gave the two solicitors permission to go into the accused's cell rather than leaving them to conduct their interview through the covered slot in the metal door.

The door was unlocked with caution, but as it swung open, it was apparent that no one need fear violence from the inmate.

Hugo sat on the bed, looking straight at the wall ahead of him. He did not stir as the genuine and false solicitors were ushered in or as the door clanged shut and was locked behind them.

"How are you feeling?" asked Gerald with professional joviality.

"All right," came the toneless reply.

"Headache better?"

"Yes, thank you."

Charles took the moment for his revelation. Perhaps it would be the necessary shock to shake Hugo out of his lethargy. "Look, it's me—Charles."

"Hello." The response was again without animation. Without even surprise.

Unwilling to lose his coup, Charles continued, "I came in under cover of Gerald's outfit."

The solicitor winced predictably at the final word. To gain another predictable wince and maybe to shift Hugo's mood by humor, Charles added, "There's no substitute for knowing a bent lawyer."

Gerald's reaction was as expected; Hugo still gave none. Charles changed tack. "Look, Hugo, I know this is one hell of a situation and I feel partly responsible for it, because I'm sure if I hadn't said certain things in my statement, you wouldn't be here and—"

Hugo cut him off, which at least demonstrated that he was taking in what was being said. But the voice in which he spoke remained lifeless. "Charles, if it hadn't been you, it would have been someone else. You only told them the truth and that was all they needed."

"Yes, but—"

"So there's no need for you to feel guilty about me or feel you have to make quixotic gestures and come down here to save me from a terrible miscarriage of justice. I don't blame you. I'm the only person to blame, if blame is the right word."

"What, you mean you think you killed her?"

"That's what I told the police."

"You've confessed?"

"Yes."

Charles looked at the solicitor. Gerald shrugged. "I didn't tell you because you didn't ask. You swept me along with some wild scheme of your own and—"

"But, Hugo, is it true?"

"Oh, Charles." The voice was infinitely weary. "I've spent some days going through this, both on my own and with the police. And . . . yes, I think I did it."

"But you can't remember?"

"Not the exact details. I know I staggered back from the Backstagers when the bar closed and I was full of hatred for Charlotte and drunk out of my mind. The next thing I remember with any clarity is waking up on the sitting room floor on Tuesday morning with the feeling that I'd done something terrible."

"But everyone feels like that when they've had a skinful."

Hugo ignored him. "It's no secret that Charlotte and I hadn't been getting on too well, that . . . the magic had gone out of our marriage. . . ." For the first time, there was slight intonation, a hint of bitterness as he spoke the cliché. "And it's no secret that I'd started drinking too much and that when I drank, we fought. So I imagine it's quite possible that, if I met her, smashed out of my mind, on Monday night, I laid hands on her and . . ." In spite of the detachment with which he was speaking, he was unable to finish the sentence.

"But you can't remember doing it?"

"I can't remember anything when I'm that smashed."

"Then why did you confess to killing her?"

"Why not? It fits the facts remarkably well. The motivation was there, the opportunity. I think my guilt is a reasonable deduction."

"Did the police put pressure on you to—"

"No, Charles. For Christ's sake—" He mastered this momentary lapse of control. "I reached the conclusion on my own, Charles. I was under no pressure." Realizing the irony of his last remark, he laughed a little laugh that was almost a sob.

"So you are prepared to confess to a murder you can't even remember just because the facts fit?"

Gerald came in at this juncture with the legal viewpoint. "I think this may be one of the most fruitful areas for the defence, actually. If you really can't remember, of course we won't be able to get you off the murder charge and that's mandatory life, but the judge might well make some recommendation and you could be out in eight years."

"You're talking as though his guilt were proven, Gerald."

"Yes, Charles. To my mind—"

"For Christ's sake, both of you shut up! What does it matter? What's the difference?"

Charles came in, hard. "The difference is, that if you are found guilty of murder, you'll be put away for life. And if you are not found guilty...." He petered out.

"Exactly." It was only then that Charles realized the depths of Hugo's despair. His friend was bankrupt of any kind of hope. It made little difference whether he spent the rest of his life in prison or at large. Except if he were free, drink might help him shorten his sentence.

Gerald got to his feet in an official sort of way. "You see, Charles, I didn't really think there was much point in your coming down here. I'm afraid it's an open-and-shut case. All we can do is to ensure that it's as well presented as possible. Actually, Hugo, I wanted to discuss the matter of instructing counsel. I felt—"

"Stop, Gerald, stop!" Charles also stood up. "We can't just leave it like this. I mean, as long as there's even a doubt...."

"I'm afraid a signed confession doesn't leave much room for doubt. Now come on, Charles, I've taken a foolish risk in bringing you down here; I think we should move as soon as possible and—"

"No, just a minute. Hugo, please, just look at me and

tell me that you did it, tell me that you strangled Charlotte, and I'll believe you."

Hugo looked at Charles. The eyes were still dull, but somewhere deep down there was a tiny spark of interest. "Charles, I can't say that definitely, because I can't remember. But I think there's a strong chance that I killed Charlotte."

"And you're prepared to leave it like that?"

Hugo shrugged. "What's the alternative? I don't see that it's going to be possible to prove that I didn't."

"Then we'll just have to prove that someone else did." The remark came out with more crusading fervor than Charles had intended.

It affected Hugo. A new shrewdness came into his eyes. "Hmm. Well, if you think that's possible, then you have my blessing to investigate until you're blue in the face."

The new animation showed how little Hugo had even considered the possibility of his innocence. Whether from his own remorse or because of the promptings of C.I.D. men anxious to sew up the case, he had not begun to think of any alternative solution.

But the shift of mood did not last. Hugo dropped back into dull despair. "Yes, if it'll amuse you, Charles, investigate everything. I'd like to feel I could be of use to someone, if only as something to investigate. And if you can't clear *my besmirched name*"—the italics were heavy with sarcasm—"then take up another hobby. Amateur dramatics, maybe?"

Gerald got purposeful again. "Charles, I think Hugo and I—"

"Just a minute. Hugo, I've got to ask you a couple of things."

"Okay." The voice had reverted to tonelessness.

"You said the other evening that Charlotte was having an affair. Do you know who her lover was?"

"Oh God, here we go again. I've been through all this with the police and—"

"Look, Charles, I don't *think*—" Gerald butted in

instinctively to defend his client.

"No, it's all right, Gerald. I can go through it once again. No, Charles, I don't know who Charlotte's lover was. No, I'm not even certain that she was having an affair. It just seemed a reasonable assumption—like so much else."

"What led you to that assumption?"

"She was a young, attractive woman. She was trapped in a marriage that was getting nowhere. She was bored, lonely. I spent more and more time out getting pissed. If she didn't start something up, then she had less initiative than I gave her credit for."

"But you had no proof?"

"What sort of proof do you want? No, I never caught her in *flagrante delicto*, no, I never saw her with a man, but if coming in at all hours, if going out on unexplained errands during the day, if saying she didn't have to stay with me, she could go elsewhere . . . if that kind of thing's proof, then I had it."

"But you never asked her directly?"

"No. Towards the end we didn't talk too much. Only to make domestic arrangements or to shout at each other. Oh, I'm sure she had a man somewhere."

"When did you start to think this?"

"I don't know. Two, three months back."

"Round the time she started rehearsing *The Seagull*."

"Possibly. And, in answer to your next question, no, I have no idea whether she was having an affair with any of the Backstagers. I just felt she was having an affair with someone." Hugo's voice was slurred with fatigue. Charles could feel Gerald's protective restlessness and knew he hadn't got much longer for his questioning.

"Hugo, I'll leave you now. Just one last thing. I want to find out more about Charlotte. Did she have any friends I could talk to, to ask about her?"

Hugo replied flatly, "No, no friends in Breckton. No close friends. That's what she always complained about.

That's why she joined the Backstagers, to meet people. No, no friends, except lover boy."

"Didn't she keep in touch with people she'd known before you married?"

"One or two. Not many. Diccon Hudson she used to see sometimes. And there was a girl she'd been at drama school with, used to come round sometimes. Not recently. I didn't like her much. Too actressy, hippy . . . young maybe is what I mean."

"What's her name?"

"Sally Radford."

"Thank you. I will go now, Hugo. I'm sorry to have to put you through it all again. But if there's a chance of finding something out, it'll be worth it."

Hugo spoke with his eyes closed. His voice was infinitely tired. "I wouldn't bother, Charles. I killed her."

Nine...

CHARLES SAT OVER a pint in the bay window of a coach lamp and horse brasses pub and looked out at the main shopping street of Breckton.

It was dominated by a long parade of shops with flats overhead, built in the thirties by some neat planning mind which had decreed that this would be enough, that there was room here for a baker, a butcher, a grocer, a greengrocer, a fishmonger, an ironmonger and one of everything else that the area might need. It would all be neat, all contained, all readily accessible.

Maybe it had had five years of this neat, ordered appearance. But soon shops had changed hands or identities and the uniformity of the original white-lettered names had been broken down by new signs and fascias. Now the line above the shop-windows was an uneven chain of oblongs in neon and garish lettering. And the frontages of the flats had been variously painted or pitted with the acne of pebbledash.

The original parade had quickly proved inadequate to

the demands of the growing dormitory suburb. New rows of shops had sprung up to flank it, each date-stamped by design, and each with its uniformity broken in the same way.

As the final insult to symmetry, opposite the old parade an enormous supermarket had been built in giant Lego bricks.

The street was crowded with shoppers. Almost all women with children. Outside the pub Charles saw two young mothers, each with a child swinging on the end of one arm and another swaddled in a baby buggy, stop and chat. And he began to feel the isolation of Charlotte in this great suburban incubator.

The whole place was designed for young couples with growing families and all the daytime social life revolved around children.

What could a girl like Charlotte have done all day in a place like this? Little more than a girl when she married, she had presumably come from some sort of lively flat life in London. The shock of her lonely incarceration in the suburbs must have been profound.

What had she done all day? At first there had been thoughts of her continuing her acting career, but, as time went on, the terrible slump of unemployment which all young actors go through while they are building up their contacts must have extended hopelessly to the point where she lost those few contacts she had. Hugo, while probably not actively discouraging her career, had come from nearly twenty years of marriage to a woman who had done nothing but minister to him and, however vehement his protests that his second marriage was going to be totally different from his first, was too selfish to give real encouragement to something that could take his new wife away from home. So Charlotte's horizons were limited before the marriage had gone sour.

What had gone wrong with the marriage? Charles felt he knew. Something comparable had happened to him. With a mental blush he remembered himself equally dewy-eyed two years before, equally certain that a young girl called Anna could put the clock back for him, that he could fall in love like an adolescent in a romantic novel. In his case, the disillusionment had been rapid and total, but he could still feel the pain of it.

With Hugo the realization must have been slower, but even more devastating. As the relationship progressed, he must have understood gradually that he had not married a goddess, only a girl. She wasn't a symbol of anything, just a real person, with all the attendant inadequacies and insecurities. Even her beauty was transient. In the short years of their marriage, he must have seen her begin to age, seen the crinkles spread beneath her eyes and know that nothing had changed, that he was the same person, growing older yoked to a different woman. And a woman in many ways less suitable than the wife he had left for her.

No doubt the sexual side of the marriage had also palled. Charles knew too well the anxieties men of his age were prey to. Perhaps Hugo had left Alice when their sex-life had started to fail, making the common male mistake of blaming the woman. He had married Charlotte as the new cure-all and then, slowly, slowly found that all the old anxieties had crept back and left him no better off than before.

Once the marriage had started to go wrong, deterioration would have been rapid. Hugo had always had the ability to shrink back into himself. No doubt when love's young dream began to crack, he didn't talk to Charlotte about it. He probably ceased to talk to her at all, morbidly digging himself into his own disappointment. He took to drinking more, arriving home later, leaving her longer and longer on her own. Again the question—what did she find to do all day?

Charles decided that was the first thing for him to find out. And he knew where to start. Still in his pocket was the spare key which Hugo had pressed on him so hospitably. He set off towards the Meckens' house.

The road of executive residences was almost deserted. Distantly an old lady walked a dog. The houses looked asleep, their net curtains closed like eyelids.

Charles felt chilly as he crunched across the small arc of gravel in front of Hugo's house. There was a strong temptation to look round, to see if he was observed, but he resisted it. There was no need to be surreptitious; he was not doing anything wrong.

Inside everything was tidy. Very different from the Tuesday night. The police had been through every room, checking, searching. And they had replaced everything neatly. Too neatly. The house looked like a museum.

He didn't know what he was looking for, but it was something to do with Charlotte. Something that would explain her, maybe even answer the nagging question of how she spent her time. He had thought he understood her in the Backstagers' car park on the Saturday night, but it was only since her death that he was beginning to feel the complexity of her character and circumstances.

Like the Winters, Hugo and Charlotte had had the luxury of space in a house designed for a family. Their double bed was in the large front bedroom, which had a bathroom en suite. But when Charles had come to stay with them for the first time, some three months before, Hugo had slept in one of the small back bedrooms and used the main bathroom. Husband and wife lived in a state of domestic apartheid.

The bed in the mistitled master bedroom was strangely pathetic. It was large with a white fur cover, a defiant sexual status symbol. It had been bought for a new, hopeful marriage, a marriage that was going to work. But now the pillows were only piled on one side and one of the bedside tables was empty.

He looked through the books on the other side. Nothing unexpected in Charlotte's literary taste. A few thrillers, a Gerald Durrell, a copy of *The Seagull*. All predictable enough.

On the shelf below was something more interesting. A copy of a Family Health Encyclopaedia. It was not a new book, printed in the fifties, probably something Hugo had brought from his previous married home. Not a great work of medical literature, but useful for spot diagnosis of childish ailments.

But why was Charlotte reading it? Was she ill? And why was she reading it in a slightly surreptitious way, half-hiding the book. Surely, if she thought she were really ill, she'd have gone to a doctor. Or at least consulted some more detailed medical work. Unless it had been the only work of reference to hand. Unless she had a panic about something she didn't dare to discuss. . . .

Good Lord, had Charlotte been worried that she was pregnant? Suddenly the thought seemed attractively plausible. A lot of what she had said in the Backstagers' car park would be explained if that were the case. That business about being off alcohol. It could be checked through the police post mortem. Mental note to ask Gerald.

If she were pregnant, a whole new volume of possible motives for killing her was opened. He felt a catch of excitement.

He tried the drawer next. That didn't seem to offer anything unexpected. A couple of rings, a broken string of beads, no doubt awaiting mending, a polythene bag of cotton wool balls, a nail-file, an empty key-ring, a jar of nail polish and . . . what was that at the back? He pulled it out. A small book covered in red leather.

It was a Roman Catholic missal. Inside the cover was written, "To Charlotte. On the occasion of her first communion, with love from Uncle Declan and Auntie Wyn."

Yes, of course, the Northern Irish background. Good little Catholic girl. Which might raise problems if she had got herself pregnant. And moral issues over contraception. Difficult to know how strong the Catholic influence would have remained. She had married Hugo in spite of his divorce. But Charles had gathered from his friend's unworthy ramblings in the Trattoria that she had let Hugo take the responsibility for birth control in the relationship. Which might mean that Charlotte would be in danger of getting pregnant if she started sleeping with someone else. Which would make sense.

He opened the fitted wardrobe on Charlotte's side of the room. The sight of her fashionable clothes gave him a sharp pang. She had worn them so well, been so beautiful. And now they hung lifeless, misshapen by the bony shoulders of the clotheshangers.

Charles ruffled through the dresses and looked with care among the litter of shoes in the bottom of the wardrobe. He still didn't know what he was looking for, but he didn't feel the time was wasted. Somehow, among her things, he felt closer to Charlotte, closer to understanding what had been going through her mind in the days before her death.

Her clothes smelt strongly of her scent, as if she were still alive. He wouldn't have been surprised to see her walk in through the door.

The wardrobe revealed nothing unexpected. Nor did the rows of drawers which flanked it. He was about to start looking round the bathroom when he stopped. There had been nothing unexpected among her clothes, but equally there had not been something that might have been expected there either.

Charlotte Mecken had been strangled with a scarf. Hugo had identified it as her own scarf and yet there were no others among her clothes. There were any number of dresses, skirts and shirts for her to choose from, any number of pullovers and pairs of shoes. But only one scarf.

When he came to think of it, Charles realized he had never seen Charlotte wearing a scarf. And what was more, even his sketchy knowledge of current fashion told him that scarves were not "in." Certainly not those crude Indian prints like the one he had seen knotted around Charlotte's neck. No, those had had a vogue in the late sixties, they now looked rather dated. Charlotte, with her sharp fashion sense, would not have been. . . . He smiled wryly as his mind formed the phrase "been seen dead in one."

What it meant was that Charlotte was most unlikely to have been wearing the scarf with which she was killed. Which made the accepted picture of the murder, of Hugo reaching out to her in a drunken fury and throttling her, unlikely. Whoever killed Charlotte must have gone to get the scarf with which to do it.

The bathroom did not offer much space for secrets. The pale green bath, basin, bidet and lavatory were modern and functional. Fluffy yellow towels hung from the heated rail. Only the mirror-fronted cabinet gave any opportunity for concealment.

The contents were predictable. Make-up, various creams, nail scissors, a tin of throat sweets, shampoo, an unopened box of Tampax, cough medicine, a roll of sticking plaster.

The decor of the bathroom was recent. The walls were olive green and the floor was covered with the same mustardy carpet as the bedroom. It was all very neat, very attractive, like a picture out of *Homes and Gardens*.

The only blemishes were two small screw-holes above the cabinet. It must have been set too high initially and been moved down to the right level for Charlotte. Maybe it had been moved when Hugo exiled himself to the other bedroom and bathroom.

Now it had been moved down, the cabinet's bottom edges rested on the top row of white tiles which surrounded the wash-basin. As a result it was tilted slightly and there was a narrow triangle of space between it and the wall.

Charles knew there would be something in there. He didn't know why. It was part of the understanding he was beginning to feel for Charlotte. She had been so young, so young, almost childlike in some respects. It was in character for her to have a hiding place for her secret things, like a girl at boarding school making one little corner of total privacy that the teachers would never know about. It was a way of maintaining her identity in a challenging situation.

Charles pressed his face to the wall and squinted along the gap. Then, very calmly, he fished in with a pen and slid out a brown envelope. It was not sealed. As he raised it to shake out the contents, the front door-bell rang.

He shoved the envelope in his pocket and swallowed his first impulse to run and hide. After all, he wasn't doing anything wrong. Hugo had given him the key without prompting. He wasn't even trespassing on his friend's property.

He tried to calm himself with such thoughts as he walked sedately downstairs, but he still felt as guilty as a schoolboy caught with an apple in his hand in an orchard.

This mood was intensified when the opened front door revealed a uniformed policeman.

"Good afternoon, sir," said the policeman in a tone that indicated that he was prepared to start quite reasonably, but was ready to get tough when the need arose.

"Good afternoon," Charles echoed foolishly.

"Might I ask what you're doing here, sir?"

"Yes, certainly," Charles affected man-of-the-world affability, to which the policeman seemed immune. "My name's Charles Paris. I'm a friend of Hugo Mecken. I've stayed here a few times. He gave me a key, actually." Charles reached into his pocket as if to demonstrate until he realized the fatuity of the gesture. "Said I could drop in any time."

"I see, sir." The policeman's tone remained reasonable, but it had a strong undercurrent of disbelief. "Rather an unusual time to drop in, sir. Or haven't you heard what's been happening here?"

"Oh yes, I know all about it," Charles replied eagerly and, as he said it, recognized his stupidity. If he'd claimed ignorance of the whole affair, he could just have walked away.

"I see, sir. In fact, we had a call from someone in the road who had seen you go into the house and who thought, under the circumstances, it was rather odd."

Good God, you couldn't blow your nose in Breckton without someone seeing. There must be watchers behind every curtain. Time for a tactical lie. "In fact, officer, the reason I am here is that, as I say, I stayed with the Meckens a few times and on the last occasion Mrs. Mecken was good enough to wash out a couple of shirts for me. Now all this terrible business has happened, I thought I'd better pick them up without delay."

The policeman seemed to accept this. "And have you found them?"

"Found what? Oh, the shirts—no, I haven't yet. I've been looking around, but I'm not sure where Mrs. Mecken would have put them."

"Ah. Well. Would you like me to accompany you round the house while you find them?" It was phrased as a question, but it wasn't one.

Like Siamese twins they went through the house. They looked in the airing cupboard, they looked in the wardrobes. Eventually Charles produced the solution he had been desperately working out for the last few minutes. "Do you know, I think Mrs. Mecken must have mixed them up with her husband's clothes and put them away in his drawer."

"Well, sir, I dare say you'll want to be off now."

Charles didn't argue.

"And, sir, I think, if you don't mind, you'd better give me that key. I'll see that it gets put with the rest of Mr. Mecken's belongings. I think, under the circumstances, with the possibility of further police investigations, the less people we have walking around this property, the better. I quite understand why you came in, sir, but if a key like this got into the wrong hands...well, who knows, it might be awkward."

"Of course." Charles had no alternative but to hand it over.

"Thank you, sir." The policeman ushered him out of the front door and closed it behind them. Then he stood in the middle of the doorstep. "Goodbye, sir."

Charles walked across the gravel and along the road in the direction of the station, conscious of the policeman's eyes following him. He wasn't going to get another chance to get inside that house without breaking and entering.

Still, the search had not been fruitless. In his pocket there was an envelope.

Ten ...

"YOU REALIZE IT'S probably illegal," said Gerald grumpily. "It's withholding evidence ... or stealing evidence or ... I'm sure there's something they could get you for."

Gerald was being unhelpful over the whole thing. He didn't want to hear how Charles had spent the rest of the morning and manifested the minimum of interest in his findings. Also it was clear that he didn't like having his friend round the Grosvenor Street office. Charles Paris was a reminder of the Mecken case and Gerald didn't want to be reminded. He wanted to reimmerse himself in his regular work, wrangling over small clauses in film and television contracts, or even sorting out the odd divorce. Having clients charged with murder upset him; he thought it was irresponsible and didn't want to dwell on it.

"I don't care," said Charles, "I think it's important. I had a look at the book on the train, but couldn't make much of it, so I thought two heads might be better than one. You always said you wanted to be included in any of my cases."

"Charles, there is a difference between what one does professionally and what one does as a hobby." Gerald could be insufferably stuffy.

"Murder's a funny sort of thing to have as a hobby. Anyway, just give me five minutes of your time to look at this stuff and then I'll leave you alone." Gerald looked dubious. "Good God, do I have to pay for your time?"

This at least brought a smile to Gerald's lips. "You'd never be able to afford my rates, Charles."

He took advantage of the shift of mood to redirect attention to the envelope on the desk. He shook it and out came a thin, blue-covered book and a beige plastic envelope. "Let's concentrate on the diary first."

He flicked through the pages. Gerald, in spite of himself, craned over to look. "Not much in it, Charles."

"No, that's what makes it interesting. Why make such a palaver about hiding a book that contains so little information?"

"Presumably because the little information it does contain is extremely secret."

"Yes. In other words, it had to be kept secret from Hugo. I mean, there was no one else in the house to hide things from, was there?"

"No."

"The interesting thing is that there's nothing at all until May. Then we have this entry—Saturday May 23rd, Backstagers' Party. Now I know that Charlotte hadn't been a member of the society long, so I reckon that could well have been her first contact.

"Seems reasonable, but it doesn't get us far."

"No. Then we get these four dates in early June—*Seagull* auditions. That's self-explanatory. And isn't it typical of that Backstagers lot to make a big production out of it and have four whole evenings of auditions.

"As we know, Charlotte was successful in the audition, because then in July we start getting rehearsals marked. Okay, that makes sense. She started the diary when she started getting involved in amateur dramatics."

"Not really something you'd treat as a big secret, is it, Charles?"

"No, the secret bit comes later. But there's something odd about this diary even from what we've seen so far. I mean, I can understand why she enters all the rehearsals—they're quite complicated and she'd need to make a note of them—but why are there no engagements before the Backstagers' party? I'm not going to believe that was the first time she went out in the year."

"No." Gerald sounded as if he was losing interest again.

Charles picked up the pace. "I think I know what it was. Not the first time she had gone out, but the first time she had arranged to go out herself. So far as I can tell, it was round that time that she and Hugo ceased to communicate. I think starting this diary was an identity thing for her. All right, if Hugo and I are not having a life together, I'll damned well make a life of my own. And this little diary was a symbol of that determination, of her separateness. And if that's why she started the diary, it explains the later entries. The Affair." He pronounced it portentously to whet Gerald's appetite. "Look."

Starting late August, in the midst of all the *Seagull* rehearsals, there was a new series of notes. Lunchtimes. 1.0—Waterloo. 1.0—Charing Cross. 1.0—Charing Cross again, then back to Waterloo. A whole sequence of them.

The last was different. It was for the Tuesday of that week. 1.0—Victoria. But that was one railway station rendezvous Charlotte Mecken did not make. Because by then she was dead.

"You reckon it was a lover?"

"It would fit rather cosily, wouldn't it, Gerald?"

"But I thought you were working on the idea that she was having an affair with someone in the Backstagers. Surely that'd be strictly local."

"Not if they wanted any degree of privacy. To have an affair in a place like Breckton would be like having it off in the middle of Wembley Stadium on Cup Final day."

"Hmm. So you reckon it was someone who worked in Town."

"Which would apply to every man in Breckton."

"Yes. It still seems odd to me that she should write all these things down. Surely it was courting disaster. I mean, if Hugo had found this book...."

"I think that danger was part of the excitement. Anyway, it would have been just as damning if Hugo had found these." Charles indicated the small beige plastic envelope.

Gerald picked it up and slid out a rectangle of foil round the edge of which was a line of transparent blisters, some of which contained small white pills. The solicitor looked up blankly. "What is it?"

Charles laughed. "Oh Gerald, what touching naïvete. Have you never seen these before? Or course, they're not really of our generation. We and our wives and girl friends did not have such modern conveniences at our disposal."

Gerald colored. "You mean these are contraceptive pills?"

"Exactly." Charles couldn't resist a little further tease. "I think that's a very heart-warming comment on your marriage, Gerald. That you shouldn't even recognize these new-fangled inventions. Fidelity is not dead. If you'd spent as much time as I have hopping in and out of unsuitable young women's bedrooms, you'd know sure enough what—"

Gerald was not amused. "I think you'd better put them away, Charles. Polly might come in."

"You're beautifully old-fashioned, Gerald. I rather think Polly would recognize them."

Gerald took refuge in a look at his watch. "Look, I've got rather a lot to get on with."

"Okay. I'll stop sending you up and be quick. These pills are the final proof that Charlotte was having an affair. Not only because of the way in which they were hidden, but because I happen to know that Hugo was in favor of more primitive methods of contraception."

Gerald's eyes opened wide. "How on earth do you know that? It's hardly the sort of thing you'd talk about."

Charles laughed again at his friend's sedateness. "He did mention it actually. But look, that's not the only thing these pills tell us. There's something else strange about them. Look."

Gerald cast an embarrassed eye over the foil and shrugged. "Don't see anything."

"The last pill was taken on a Wednesday."

"So?" Gerald was looking distinctly uncomfortable. The conversation was straying beyond the boundaries of what he considered suitable masculine subject matter.

"Charlotte was killed on Monday night and yet the last pill was taken on a Wednesday. It wasn't the end of her cycle because there are still pills left. So it means that she stopped taking the pills at least five days before she died."

"Maybe she just forgot them." Gerald's interest was beginning to overcome his embarrassment.

"Unlikely. Though I suppose she was very tied up with the play and it's possible. But you would have thought a married woman in the middle of an affair would be extra careful."

"Unless the affair had broken up and she no longer had any use for the pills..."

"That's a thought. That *is* a thought." The existence of a jilted lover opened new vistas of motivation. But there was a snag. "On the other hand, if we look back at the diary, there's that Victoria assignation for the Tuesday, not to mention a Charing Cross one for the Monday. Which rather suggests that the affair was still swinging along. So that can't be why she stopped taking the pills."

The flow of logic had stopped. Charles sighed. He was buzzing round something important, but he hadn't found it yet. He had got the right pieces, but he wasn't putting them in the right order. "Oh well, I suppose the first thing is to find out who the lover was."

"I should think, if he exists, the police would know by now."

"Do you reckon?"

"Of course. They're not stupid. Maybe you can keep that sort of thing secret from the nosey parkers of Breckton, but the police can go around and question everyone who knew Charlotte, they can talk to the railway staff who saw her travelling up on her assignations, all that sort of thing."

"Yes. Well, if the police happen to tell you who the lover was—or any other useful snippets of information, you will pass them on, won't you?"

"If they are the sort of things I think I should pass on, yes."

Charles had an urge to punch Gerald right in the middle of his formal solicitor's face, but he decided it wasn't worth losing friends that way. "Maybe I'd better go."

"Yes. I am meant to be getting on with my work. I do have clients depending on me, you know."

"Yes, I'm sure we can depend that one of them is paying for your time at the moment."

Gerald didn't rise to the running joke.

There was a copy of *Spotlight* in the outer office where Gerald's secretary Polly sat. Charles picked up *Actresses L-Z.*

Sally Radford was under *Juvenile and Juvenile Character.* The photograph showed a strong face dominated by a largish nose. Straight dark hair parted in the middle and looped back like curtains behind the ears. It was one of those faces which in the flesh would either look very attractive or not quite make it. Depend to some extent on the coloring. Beneath the black and white photograph it said "5ft. 6in." and "Blue Eyes." The blue eyes were unexpected and promising.

There was no name and number for an agent. Just "c/o

Spotlight" as a contact. That was revealing to Charles as an actor. Probably meant she had not yet got very far in her career and either couldn't find an agent willing to represent her until she had more experience or had decided that for the moment she was going to do as well finding work for herself. It also probably meant that she was based in London rather than doing a season out at some provincial rep. If she were out of town she'd want an agent as a point of contact for inquiries.

Polly graciously granted him the use of her phone and he got through. The girl on the *Spotlight* switchboard said that Sally Radford was likely to be ringing in and could he leave a number where he could be contacted? He explained that that was rather difficult as he wasn't sure of his movements.

"Is it important?" asked the girl, meaning "Is it work?"

"Yes, it is," Charles replied, glad that she'd phrased it in a way that enabled him to reply without lying.

"Okay then, I can give you a number to contact her."

"Thank you very much."

Sally Radford answered straight away. Her voice was husky and well-articulated without being actressy. It confirmed the strength of character implicit in the photograph.

"Hello, my name's Charles Paris. I got your name through *Spotlight*."

"Yes."

He heard the catch of excitement in her voice and realized that that was a rotten way to introduce himself to an out-of-work actress. He had better disillusion her quickly. "Sorry, it's not about work."

"Oh." The disappointment could not be disguised.

"No, I'm sorry, it's a rather awkward thing I'm ringing about. I believe you were a friend of Charlotte Mecken."

"Yes." The voice went serious. Charles began to think that she was probably a talented actress; her inflections on small words were telling. She continued, not playing it tragic queen, just sad, "I thought somebody might be in touch. I suppose I was her closest friend—though with Charlotte that did not necessarily mean very close. Are you police?"

"No, I'm not actually. I'm a . . ." He resisted the temptation to say "private investigator," which was a bit grandiose for what he was doing and probably an offence under the Trades Descriptions Act. ". . . friend of Hugo's."

"Ah." Again the intonation was informative and reminded him that Hugo and Sally had not got on well.

"As you probably know, Hugo's been arrested for murder. . . ."

"Yes."

"Well, I'm by no means certain that he's guilty. That's why I'd like to meet you and talk if I may."

"Sure. Anything I can do to help."

"Can we meet soon?"

"Soon as you like. I don't have a lot happening at the moment." The understatement spoke of some weeks of sitting by the telephone.

Charles arranged to go round to her flat in Maida Vale at six and put the phone down with the small satisfaction of having made a date.

Eleven . . .

SALLY RADFORD DID look better in color than in monochrome. The strength of the face and its potential hardness were made less daunting by the piercing blue of her eyes. She was dressed in a collarless man's shirt with a brown stripe, well-cut jeans and cowboy boots. Almost flat-chested, but very feminine. A hint of some musky scent.

Her flat showed the same kind of style. Obviously rented furnished, but with sufficient touches of her own to take the curse off the Indentikit furniture. A Japanese paper kite in the shape of a bird dangled over the fireplace. Tall grasses in the old green bottle balanced the slumped display of books on a low shelf. The decor was minimal, but assured.

The girl emanated the same confidence. Not the go-getting brashness that Charles had encountered in so many young actresses, but an inner patience, an impression that everything she did was logical and right.

Charles found her relaxing. Partly because of her

directness, but also because she was an actress, a real actress to whom he could talk about the theatre without fearing the stupid or exaggerated responses he had come to expect from the Backstagers. It was only as he talked to her that he realized how long it was since he had been with real actors.

She sat him down and offered him tea or coffee. He chose tea, which came in a blue and grey earthenware mug. China with lemon. Good.

"Okay, what do you want me to tell you?" Down to business as soon as the social formalities had been observed.

"Let me fill you in a bit on what I'm doing first. I was with Hugo when he found Charlotte's body. . . ." He then filled her in on the background of Hugo's confession and his own reasons for believing that it was not necessarily conclusive.

Sally was silent for a moment, then made up her mind. "Okay, let's accept your hypothesis for the time being. What can I do for you?"

"Just a few questions about Charlotte. I'm sorry, I know you didn't like Hugo, but I would like to clear up—"

"I didn't dislike him. I don't think he even disliked me. I think he just resented my friendship with Charlotte. Partly because he was jealous of what he imagined to be our closeness—he was terribly aware of their age difference and was afraid of Charlotte seeing too much of her contemporaries in case they took her away from him—which is ironic, seeing how the marriage turned out. Also I'm an actress and I tended to talk about the theatre. I don't think Hugo really wanted Charlotte's career to develop, in case that took her away from him."

"That's rather what I thought."

"So he got very uptight if I started talking about contacts or auditions coming up or prospects for jobs or. . . . Though," she added on a personal note of bitterness, "I don't think he need have worried if Charlotte's success had been anything like mine over the last couple of years."

"Work not coming?"

She shook her head wryly. "You're a master of understatement. No, I'm not exactly fighting the offers away from my door. I've had a few radios, one or two close calls on West End auditions, but...." She straightened up. "But you know all that. It's familiar country."

"Right." There was a pause of great togetherness, of shared experience. "I don't know Charlotte well, Sally. I only really met her through Hugo and, you know, you view your friend's wives and girl friends through a kind of refracting glass of the friends themselves. What I've been trying to do since Charlotte was killed is to see her on her own, to know what her own personality was like, apart from Hugo. What I really want you to do is tell me if I'm on the right lines in understanding her, or if I'm hopelessly wrong."

"How do you see her?"

"It's funny, I keep coming back to the image of her as terribly young. I don't mean just in age. I mean young for her years. Immature even."

Sally nodded slowly. "That's quite shrewd. Yes, she was. I knew her right through drama school and she was always very naïve, sort of wide eyed about things. She never looked it. So beautiful, for a start, and she had such superb dress sense that everyone thought she was the ultimate sophisticated woman, but it was only a front—no, not even a front, because she didn't put it up consciously. It was when I realized this that I first started to like her. Suddenly I saw that she wasn't a daunting, challenging woman, but just a rather earnest child. I think we're always drawn to people by knowledge of their weaknesses. It's so comforting, that moment when you realize that you don't have to be afraid and competitive any more.

"I think Charlotte had had a very sheltered upbringing. Northern Ireland. Straight-laced, inward-looking family so far as I can gather. Convent education."

"It seems odd, Sally, considering that, that she was

allowed to go to drama school. You'd think there would have been family opposition."

"Yes, it was strange. But she was strong-minded about certain things. And she knew she could act and that that was what she wanted to do. I don't think anyone could cross her once she'd really made up her mind about something."

"Hmm. She was a good actress. I only saw her in one thing, tatty amateur production of *The Seagull*, but by God it was all there."

"Oh yes, she was good. That's what made her marrying Hugo so sad. He didn't want her to be a successful actress. He was miserly about her, wanted to keep her to himself."

"Do you think he even objected to her joining the amateur society?"

"I don't think he was keen. That was something she decided to do very much on her own. Anyway, he could hardly object—I gather he had been a member to take advantage of the bar for some time. But I doubt if they discussed it. By then they were hardly speaking."

Charles nodded. It was satisfying to have his diagnosis of the marriage and Charlotte's motivation confirmed. "So she joined as a deliberate attempt to assert her own individuality?"

"Yes. I think she also saw it as a step of getting herself back on the road to the professional theatre. You know how it is in the business—if you don't work for a bit, you lose confidence. I think she had to do something to prove to herself that she could still act."

"It's surprising that she started at such a local level, that she didn't just up and leave Hugo and go back to the real theatre world."

"I don't think she really wanted to leave him. She had been very much in love when they married. It was only when he withdrew completely into himself that the marriage foundered. I think she still hoped that one day he would come out of his sulk and everything would be all right again. Deep down she had a great belief in the sanctity of marriage. The Catholic background again. She wouldn't have left her husband lightly."

"Hmm. But she would have an affair with another man lightly?"

Sally Radford appraised him coolly. "You know about that then. In fact, I don't think that was entered into lightly either. Charlotte was a very serious girl—as I said, an earnest child. No, I think the affair was because she just had to do something to get out of her spiral of loneliness. And also because she was very attracted to the man in question."

"You don't, by any chance...?" Charles hazarded hopefully.

Sally shook her head. "'Fraid not. I have this sneaking feeling that she did once mention a man's name to me, but I'm sorry, I can't for the life of me remember what it was."

"But she did tell you she was having an affair?"

"Not directly. But she came to me for practical advice, and I put two and two together."

"Practical advice?"

"Yes. It's back to the naïveté we were talking about. Charlotte had always been a bit backward in sexual matters. I mean, at drama school, where all the rest of us were screwing away like rabbits, she kept herself to herself."

"You don't mean she managed to come through drama school a virgin? I thought that was a technical impossibility."

Sally smiled. "I don't know if she was actually a virgin, but I do know that she was pretty inhibited about such things. Needless to say, all the men were panting round her like puppies, but I don't know if any of them got anywhere."

"Not even Diccon Hudson?"

"Ah, you know Mr. Golden Voice. Yes, he certainly tried as hard as any of them, but I just don't know. He made a point of trying to have everything in sight, really put it about. What do they reckon that kind of manic screwing's a sign of? Latent homosexuality? Not in his case, I think."

"But did he make it with Charlotte?"

"I think probably not. And I'm sure if he didn't it made him furious. Great blow to the great pride. No, for Charlotte, Hugo was the first big thing in her life. I think perhaps she found the slower approach of the older man less frightening than the ravenous groping of her contemporaries."

"Yes, of course, we old men do slow down quite a bit," Charles agreed with mock-seriousness.

Sally Radford realized what she had said and giggled. She looked at him and a new awareness came into their conversation. "Anyway, Charles, to come up to date. . . . Some time in July, Charlotte rang and asked if we could meet for lunch. We did and, after some small talk and embarrassment on her part, she asked me how she should set about getting on the Pill. Since she had got that far into her married life without it and because she was so surreptitious about the inquiry, I reckon that that meant she had started sleeping with someone other than her husband."

"Yes, that would fit." Charles quickly summarized his discovery of the pills in their hiding place in Charlotte's bathroom.

"Anyway," Sally continued, "for some reason she didn't want to go to her local G.P. So I recommended the Brook Clinic in Totty Court Road. I'd been there myself, they're very helpful."

"So we can assume that they fitted her out and the affair continued."

"I imagine so. I found it a bit sad that she came to me actually. I mean, not that she was so ignorant, that was just part of her character, but the fact that I was the only person she could talk to. I didn't know her that well, and yet she was in a strange way dependent on me."

"Hmm. When did you last see her or hear from her?"

"We had lunch again quite soon after the time I

mentioned. Since then, just the odd phone call."

"Did she talk again about the contraception business?"

"Only once. Otherwise it was as if it had never happened."

"And the once?"

"That was quite recently. I think the last time I heard from her. She must have read some scare article about the Pill in a magazine or something. She asked all kinds of things about the dangers of it. Not straight away, but she maneuvered the conversation round to it."

"What sort of things did she ask?"

"Practically everything—about the dangers of embolism, could the Pill cause obesity, was it liable to raise the blood pressure, could it harm the foetus if a pregnant woman took it, could it lead to sterility, did it upset the cycle irrevocably—just about every Pill scare that has ever been put out, and a few old wives' tales thrown in for good measure."

"Did she sound worried?"

"She didn't actually *sound* worried, but she was a good actress and the fact that she raised the subject suggested to me that she must be."

"You didn't get any impression which of the particular dangers she was worried about?"

"'Fraid not. If there was one in particular she was asking about, she managed to put up an effective smoke-screen with all the other. I assumed that the Pill had just affected her cycle. It often does at first. If her periods had always been regular before, it would probably worry her if things suddenly got out of phase."

Charles was silent, his passivity hiding the speed with which his mind was working. There were other things that could cause an upset in a woman's cycle.

Sally Radford suddenly spoke again, with more emotion than hitherto. "God knows why she asked me. That's what I meant by being sad, that there was no one else she could ask, no family, no friendly doctor. As if I were an international expert on contraception."

The bitterness in the last sentence made Charles look up and he was surprised to see the glint of a tear in her eye.

She dashed it away. "I'm sorry. It's just that it seems so inhuman—Charlotte dead and presumably dissected on some police mortuary slab while we meticulously pick through her gynecological history."

"Yes, but there's something else worrying you, isn't there?"

She looked up at him, giving the full benefit of those blue eyes. "You're shrewd, Charles Paris. Yes, it was ironical her coming to me with her contraceptive problems. I learned the hard way."

"An abortion?"

"Yes. Sixth form at school."

"I'm sorry." He offered the useless comfort of someone who knew nothing of the circumstances.

"Oh yes." She tossed her head back to signify her return to a controlled mood. "Yes, it's not really the emotional shock in my case. It's just the fear that, you know, something might have gone wrong, that I might not be able to conceive again as a result. I mean, not that there's anyone around at the moment whose baby I want to have, but . . . I don't know, you just have this fear that if you couldn't have children, it'd warp you in some way. Oh, it's all irrational. Forget it."

Charles changed the subject, but he didn't forget it. "Sorry to have dragged you through all this, but I'm very grateful to you for giving me your time and for being so frank. Can I take you out for a drink to say thank you?"

"Why not?" She consulted her watch. "Twenty to eight. Yes, I think we can safely assume that all the major impresarios of London have packed their briefcases for the night and that I can leave the telephone unattended without jeopardizing my chances of becoming a STAR."

They went to a rather camp Victorian pub in Little Venice and drank large amounts of red wine. Then Charles took Sally to a little Italian restaurant where they drank more red wine. When he saw her back to her flat, there didn't seem to be any question of his leaving.

"Why are we going to sleep together?" asked Charles with the deep philosophy of the drunk as he hopped round the bedroom trying to get his trousers off.

"In my case," Sally replied, pulling her shirt over her head, "because I like you and on the whole I do sleep with people I like. Also . . ." She paused profoundly. "I'm after experience."

"Experience that will one day be seen in a stage performance before the paying public?"

"Maybe."

"Well, it may surprise you to know that even at my advanced age I'm still after experience." He mused. "Do you know, I'm fifty this week. Fifty."

"There, there." She took him in her arms. "Rejuvenate yourself with the body of a young woman. Like Dracula."

"You're nothing like Dracula. If you were you'd have run screaming from the garlic in the *pollo sopreso.*"

"There, there. Let's hope your body's not as decrepit as your wit. Otherwise I'm left out in the cold."

"There, there. And there." She drew in her breath sharply as he touched her. "I think you'll find all's in working order."

"Remember," she whispered as they rolled together, "no strings. Experience."

"No strings," he echoed as their bodies' heats fused.

"And no babies," she said, nimbly detaching herself and reaching into her bedside drawer. "Good God, considering our conversation, it's amazing I forgot it." She flicked the small white pill into her mouth and swallowed it down jerkily.

"Tell me . . ." Charles's mind fumbled through the fogs of alcohol. ". . . if you were having an affair with someone, what would stop you from taking your pill? Apart from just forgetting it?"

"I suppose if the bloke walked out, I might—except that I wouldn't because I always live in the hope that something else is going to come along. Or if I wanted to get pregnant—except then I'd be more likely to do it at the end of the cycle."

"Or. . . ."

"Or, I suppose, if I thought I was pregnant, I'd stop as soon as I realized . . . for fear of hurting the baby."

Charles smiled in a satisfied way as he took Sally back into his arms and crushed her flat but oh so feminine chest to his.

It was unhurried and good. As they snuggled together to sleep, Charles murmured, "It simplifies everything, doesn't it? Sex therapy. Frees the mind."

"Yes," Sally agreed lazily, "it's freed my memory."

"What do you mean?"

"I've just remembered the name that Charlotte mentioned, the guy who I think must have been her lover."

Charles was instantly alert. "Yes?"

"Does the name Geoff make any sense?"

"Yes," said Charles. "Yes, it does."

Twelve...

CHARLES GOT BACK to Hereford Road at half-past nine the next morning, feeling pretty good. So it wasn't all over; it could still happen. His mind started to generalize, filling with images of other nubile young girls through whose beds he would flit.

An envelope on the doormat quickly dislocated his mood. A birthday card. Right on cue. Friday, November 5th. The card was a well-chosen reproduction of an El Greco grandee and contained the message "Congratulations on half a century. Love, Frances." It served as a brutal reminder not only of his age but also of his neglected responsibilities. Images of future girls gave way to wistful recollection.

To stop himself getting maudlin, he brought his concentration to bear on Charlotte's murder. Now he knew the identity of her lover, the case seethed with new possibilities. The first thing he must do was to talk to Geoffrey Winter.

The sound of the phone ringing broke into his train of

thought. Expecting it would be a boyfriend of one of the beefy Swedish girls who lived in the other bedsitters, he answered. It was his agent, Maurice Skellern.

That was unusual. Maurice was terribly inefficient and never rang his clients. Since he had never got any work for them, there was no point; they could ring him to find that out.

"Charles, I've had an inquiry from an advertising agency about your availability for a voice-over."

"What, Mills Brown Mazzini?"

"No, another one."

"That's good. Hugo said that once somebody uses you in this field, you start getting lots more inquiries. Perhaps I've become Flavor of the Month."

"Well, they want you to do a voice test."

"When?"

"This morning. At eleven."

"Shee. I'd better get straight along. What's the address and who do I ask for?"

Maurice gave the details. "Incidentally, Charles, about this voice-over business. I don't know much about it. . . ."

"Well, there's an admission."

"What I was going to say was, I'm glad about all the work, but we don't seem to have had too many checks through yet."

"No, we'll have just the basic studio session fees so far. A few thirty-five quids. It's when the commercials go out and get repeated that the money really starts to flow. I mean, if this Bland compaign takes off . . . well. . . . Exclusive contract has even been mentioned. And you see, it's already leading to other inquiries."

"So you reckon there's a lot of work there?"

"Could be. Some people do dozens of voice-overs a week. Mix it in with film dubbing, reading books for the blind, other voice work. Make vast sums. Mostly people with specialist agents, of course," he added maliciously.

Maurice was too used to Charles's snide lines about

their relationship even to acknowledge this one. "Well, good, good. Obviously the right step for you career-wise. Haven't I always been telling you you should be extending your range, finding a wider artistic fulfilment?"

"No, you've always been telling me I should make more money. By the way, anything else about?"

"There's a new permanent company being set up in Cardiff. Might be worth trying for that."

"Hardly me, is it—Cardiff? Anyway, if this voice-over business gets under way, I'm going to have to be based in London for a bit. Till I've made enough to keep the taxman quiet. No nice convenient little tellies coming up, are there?"

"Haven't heard of anything. London Weekend are supposed to be setting up a new series about Queen Victoria's cooks, but I haven't heard when."

"Then let's live in hope of the voice-overs. I'd better get along to this place for the test. By the way, did they say what the product was?"

"Yes. Something for . . . depopulation, was it?"

"For depopulation? You mean, like napalm?"

"No, no. For removing unsightly hair."

"Depilation, Maurice."

The new depilatory about to be launched on the armpits of the world was called No Fuzz and the selling line was "There's no fuss with No Fuzz."

Charles used his heavy cold voice again, because that was what they wanted. (If he had to keep grinding it down like that, he was going to ruin his vocal cords.) He dropped into the routine of giving every possible intonation to the new line, waiting for the fatuous notes from the account executive in charge ("Give it a bit more *brio*, love" and "Try it with just a smidgeonette of sex in the voice") and let his mind wander. He couldn't lose the suspicion that a properly programmed computer could sew up the entire voice-over business.

He was kept for an hour, told he was super and that

they'd give him a tinkle. And he had earned another thirty-five pounds.

In the reception of the agency he met Diccon Hudson. Charles saw the other man's eyes narrow at the sight of a potential rival. Diccon worked hard to maintain all his agency contacts and wouldn't take kindly to being aced out by a non-specialist. "You up for the No Fuzz campaign?" he asked directly.

"Yes."

"Becoming rivals, aren't we. First Mr. Bland, now. . . ."

"I haven't necessarily got this one."

"No." Diccon Hudson seemed to gain comfort from the fact. His ferrety face could not conceal what was going through his mind.

Charles recalled suddenly that Diccon was on his list of people to check out in his investigation. "You heard about Charlotte?"

The name sent a spasm across Diccon's over-expressive face. "I heard. I was pretty cut up about it."

Charles nodded. "Terrible, yes. I suppose you hadn't seen her for a long time."

"I saw her quite recently actually."

"Not on Monday night, I suppose," Charles joked, to draw Diccon out.

"No, not on Monday night. I—" Diccon suddenly stopped short, as if he'd thought better of what he was going to say.

"What were you doing on Monday night then, buddy?" Charles dropped into a New York cop accent to take the curse off his interrogation.

"Nothing." Diccon hurried on, "I last saw Charlotte about a fortnight ago. We used to meet for the odd lunch."

"Regularly?" Charles was beginning to wonder if, in spite of Sally Radford's recollection of the name "Geoff," there was any connection between Diccon and the dates in Charlotte's diary.

But the theory was shattered before it was formed. "I was away in Crete for all of August, but I saw her a few

times before and after. A few times." The repeat was
accompanied by a smug smile, enigmatic, but probably
meant to be taken as a form of sexual bragging.

"Did Hugo know?"

Diccon gave a contemptuous shrug; the question
wasn't worth answering.

Now for Geoffrey Winter. Charles was glad that Sally had
come up with the name, because it confirmed a conclusion
towards which his mind had been moving.

He had decided that, if Charlotte had chosen her lover
from the ranks of the Backstagers, then Geoffrey was the
only candidate. Perhaps it was *The Seagull* which had led
him to the conclusion. Trigorin, after all, was the older
man who seduced Nina. Or maybe it was just that
Geoffrey seemed the only one of the Backstagers
sufficiently attractive and interesting to be worthy of
Charlotte.

He had first got an inkling of something between the
two of them at the cast party. Not that they had been
together; they had been apart. They had both danced so
ostentatiously, both putting on such a show with other
people. There had been something studied about the way
they had avoided each other. All of the rest of the cast had
been constantly reforming and forming in little knots to
remember some near disaster or ill-disguised corpse, but
Geoffrey and Charlotte had always ended up in different
groups.

So Charles liked to think that he would have looked up
Geoffrey's office address in the phone book even if Sally
hadn't mentioned the name.

When he did, the address gave him further confirmation. Listed under Geoffrey Winter Associates, Architects. And an office in Villiers Street, adjacent to Charing
Cross Station and just over Hungerford Bridge from
Waterloo.

The office was on the top floor. A door with a frosted
glass window bore the name on a stainless steel plaque.

He tapped on the window, but, getting no response, tried the handle.

The door was opened. He found himself in a small outer office. It was very tidy, box files upright in rows along the shelves, cardboard tubes of plans stacked on brackets on the walls. The color scheme and the choice of the sparse furniture showed the same discrimination as Geoffrey's study.

But the outer office gave no feeling of work. It was like the Meckens' house after it had been tidied by the police—too neat to be functional.

The typewriter on the desk was shrouded in its plastic cover, as if its typist had long gone. There were no coats on the row of aluminium pegs.

But there was someone in the next room. Or presumably more than one person, because Charles could hear a voice. Talking loudly, in a rather stilted way.

He drew close to the connecting door, but couldn't make out the words. He couldn't even be sure that they were in English. He tapped on the door, but there was no break in the speech. He turned the handle and pushed the door open.

There was only one person in the room. The first thing Charles saw was the soles of a new pair of shoes resting on the desk. Behind them, a pair of hands holding an Arden edition of *The Winter's Tale*. And behind that the surprised face of Geoffrey Winter.

"Good God. Charles Paris."

"Yes."

"Have you come to commission me to build a second National Theatre?"

"No such luck, I'm afraid. It's not work."

"It never is."

"Bad at the moment?"

"Not a good time for the architect on his own. No one's building anything."

"The economic situation."

"Yes."

"Like everything else. Like why theatres are cutting down on resident companies, why managements are putting on less shows. . . ."

This banter was conducted at a pleasant enough level, but they both knew that it was only a formal observance preceding something more important. Charles decided there was little to be gained by further prevarication. "I've come to talk about Charlotte Mecken."

"Ah." Geoffrey Winter tensed fractionally at the name, but he didn't give anything away. Charles got the same message that he had got from the performance as Trigorin, that here was a man of considerable emotional depth, but with great control over his reactions. He did not let anything emerge until he had fully considered how he wanted to present it.

Charles had hoped for more reaction and was thrown when he didn't get it. So he blundered on and, after a brief explanation of his belief in Hugo's innocence, asked point blank if Geoffrey had been Charlotte's lover.

The response was an "Oh," delivered absolutely flat; it gave nothing. But Geoffrey Winter was only playing the pause for maximum dramatic effect. Charles recognized the acting technique and let the silence ride. At last Geoffrey spoke.

"Well, congratulations. You've done your homework well. There's no point in my denying it, you're right. Since the police know, no doubt it'll all come out at Hugo's trial, so why should I pretend? Yes, I was Charlotte's lover until she . . . died."

He changed pace suddenly on the last word, straightened up in his chair and turned to look out over the irregular roofs of London. As if in the grip of strong emotion. Charles always found it difficult to judge with actors. Since their lives were devoted to simulation, it was often hard to distinguish when their feelings were genuine.

He didn't offer any comment; he let Geoffrey play the scene at his own pace. Sure enough, when the pause had extended far enough to make even a Pinter audience feel uncomfortable, Geoffrey turned back from the window and looked piercingly at him. "I suppose your next question is going to be—did I kill Charlotte?"

In fact, that was not where Charles's suspicions were leading, but he decided to play along with the scene. "I was going to be a bit more subtle than that."

"Well, Charles, the answer is no. I didn't kill her. It would have been perverse for me to . . . I had no cause to break up what was happening . . . about the best . . . thing that. . . ." Again he was overcome by real or simulated emotion (or, most likely, an amalgam of the two). He turned back to the window.

"I'm sorry to put you through this, Geoffrey. I realize it must be painful. But Hugo is a friend and I have to investigate every avenue."

Geoffrey was once again master of himself (if indeed he had ever relinquished control). "I quite understand. I've been through all this with the police."

"How did they find out?"

"Not difficult. They checked Charlotte's comings and goings with the staff at Breckton Station, realized the convenient position of my office for such an affair, then came and asked me, more or less as you have done. It seemed pointless to try and hide the facts. It would only have made things worse."

"Did they ask you if you'd killed her?"

"They, as you intended to be, were a bit more subtle than that. But they did ask a few pertinent questions about my movements on Monday. I think they were just checking; I didn't get the impression they had much doubt about Hugo's guilt. In fact, they came to see me after he had been arrested, so I suppose they were just building up the background to the case."

Charles must have been looking at Geoffrey quizzically, because the architect seemed to read his thoughts. He gave a dry laugh. "Yes, I'll tell you what I told the police. I'll establish my alibi for you—as I believe the saying goes.

"Part of it you know, because you were with me in the Back Room. As you recall, we left there together and walked down to the main road. Now, in case you're thinking that I might have immediately doubled back and taken the insane step of strangling someone I loved, it seems that there is proof that Charlotte was still alive and well at nine o'clock. Shad Scott-Smith, you may remember, in the Back Room buying drinks for *The Seagull* cast. Because Charlotte wasn't there, he rang her from his home at about ten to nine. He rang off at nine. The reason he could be so specific is that he heard the opening of *I, Claudius* on the telly and he wanted to watch it."

"It seems to have cut a swathe through the lives of an entire generation, that programme."

"It did. Big success. Pity you weren't in it."

"Yes, there'd be some pretty useful repeats on something like that. I'm afraid I've never been in what's been hailed as a television success."

The change of subject relaxed the tension between the two men and Geoffrey continued in almost a bantering tone. "Right, on with my alibi. I arrived home just before nine to find that Vee, as another member of the generation decimated by *I, Claudius*, was all geared up to watch. I left her to it and went upstairs to do some work on my lines for *The Winter's Tale*.

"For the next bit, I have cause to be thankful that I have a bloody-minded neighbour. Apparently, old Mrs. Withers next door, who goes to bed at about nine, could hear me ranting away through the wall—her bedroom's right next door to my study. Apparently she's not a great fan of Shakespeare and later on, when I got a bit carried away with the character, she took it upon herself to ring up the police and complain. A very apologetic constable was round at our place for some time saying that old

ladies could be very difficult. Apparently, according to
the police in the murder case, this means that I'm covered
for the time of the death."

He paused, not with satisfaction or triumph, but as if
he had reached a natural conclusion. Then he added,
"Fortunate, really. Most evenings spent at home, it would
be very difficult to account for one's movements."

"Thank you very much for going through it all again.
And for bearing with my wild accusations."

"That's quite okay. I sympathize with your motives.
I'm as keen as you are to find the person who killed
Charlotte. I just thought he had already been found."

"You may well be right. Certainly the fact that she was
having an affair would give Hugo even more of a motive.
Do you know if he knew about it?"

"No idea. Charlotte and I didn't discuss him."

"From my conversations with him, I got the impression that he thought she was having an affair, but didn't
know who with."

Geoffrey smiled painfully. "Ironic though it may seem,
Charlotte and I did try to be discreet about it. I mean,
never let on what we felt for each other round Breckton.
We didn't want to be gossip-fodder for the Backstagers."

"Very wise. So she always came up here?"

Geoffrey nodded sadly. "Yes. It started in the summer.
You remember the long, hot summer?"

This new note of wistfulness, like everything else,
sounded contrived. Charles didn't respond to it. "Tell me,
why did Charlotte come sometimes to Charing Cross and
sometimes to Waterloo?"

Geoffrey raised his eyebrows and nodded in appreciation. "Ten out of ten for homework. To answer that
question, I think you have to understand what Charlotte
was like. It was her first affair, she treated it with great
excitement, and I think much of the excitement came
from the secrecy. Coming to different stations was her
idea of discretion, of covering her tracks. She was very
young. As you see," he continued with irony, "the

smoke-screen was not very effective. It didn't take the police—or you—long to see through it."

Charles felt a glow of satisfaction for his understanding of Charlotte's character. "And was it for the same reason that she planned to go to Victoria on the day after she died?"

"Victoria?"

"I'd better explain. I found Charlotte's engagement diary down at the house. She'd listed all your meetings by a time and the name of the terminus she was coming to. The last two entries were one o'clock at Charing Cross on the Monday, the day she died, and then one o'clock on the Tuesday at Victoria."

"Ah, I didn't know she'd done that."

"What—put the places down in the book?"

"Yes. Yes, that must have been it." For the first time in their interview he seemed to be in the grip of some emotion that was more powerful than his control. "I'm sorry, it's just so typical of her, to think that that kind of subterfuge would fool anyone. Going to Victoria instead . . . I mean, to go out of her way like that to be inconspicuous and then write all the details down in a diary. I think a lot of the affair was just a game for her, like a schoolgirl having a midnight feast."

"But it was serious on your side?"

Geoffrey looked pained. "Serious on both sides— in our different ways. It was very good."

"And it was still going well when she died? I mean, you hadn't had a row or . . . ?"

Geoffrey looked at Charles with some distaste, pitying his lack of subtlety. "I know what you mean. No, we hadn't had a lover's tiff which would inspire me with hatred to go and kill her. It was all going very well." He was becoming wistful again.

"And was it going to change?"

"Change?"

"I mean, were you likely to get divorced and marry?"

Geoffrey shook his head slowly. "No, it was an affair. I

wanted to go on as long as possible, but I suppose some time it would have ended. I've had other affairs. They all end sooner or later. I wouldn't have left Vee. People can never understand how close Vee and I are. I'm just one of those men who's capable of loving more than one woman at a time. Do you understand?"

"I think I do. Did Vee know about Charlotte?"

"I assume so. I never told her, but she's not stupid."

"Didn't she get jealous?"

"Vee would only get jealous if she thought someone was likely to take me away from her. She knew that no one would. According to my own rules of morality, I'm very loyal."

Charles nodded. Geoffrey had a male chauvinist vanity which was quite strong enough to blind him to his wife's real feelings. No woman, however liberated, actually welcomes the knowledge that her husband is sleeping around. And Charles knew from the way that Vee had watched her husband at the cast party, she had a strong possessive instinct.

There wasn't a lot more Charles could find out. "I must go. I mustn't keep you from your work any longer."

Geoffrey laughed cynically and flapped his copy of *The Winter's Tale*. "Ah, my work. Geoffrey Winter Associates haven't had a decent size job now for four months."

"Where are the Associates?"

"Disassociated—or should it be dissociated? I never know. All gone their separate ways, anyway. Even the secretary's gone."

"So you just come up here and do nothing all day?"

"Sometimes things come up. Odd little jobs, through friends in various government departments. That's the answer these days—work in the public sector. No room for men on their own. I keep applying for jobs in local government and things, but as yet no luck. So I stay on here and wait. May as well, until the lease is up."

"When's that?"

"A couple of months."

"And then what?"

Geoffrey Winter's shrug started expansive as if it encompassed every possibility in the known world, but shrank down to nothing.

"So what do you live on?"

"Credit." He laughed unconcernedly. "And the confidence that something will turn up."

Charles went back to Hereford Road feeling excited. He had been glad to hear Geoffrey's watertight alibi because that removed him from the running. And enabled Charles to follow the suspicions which were hardening in his mind. It wasn't Geoffrey he suspected; it was his wife. He could not forget the tensed-up energy he had felt in Vee's body as they had danced together. She was a woman capable of anything.

The chain of motivation was simple. Vee's jealousy of Charlotte had started when she was beaten for the role of Nina which she had regarded as hers by right. It had been compounded by the discovery of her husband's affair with the upstart. That, however, she could have borne; what drove her to murder was the discovery that Charlotte was giving Geoffrey the one thing that their marriage could not—a child.

The opportunity for committing the crime was equally easily explained. Geoffrey had been at such pains to establish his own alibi that he hadn't thought about his wife's. While he was upstairs ranting through Leontes, she was assumed to be downstairs watching *I, Claudius*. So far as Geoffrey was concerned, that was what she was doing. He could presumably hear the television from upstairs.

But a television set conducts a one-way conversation, regardless of whether or not there is anyone watching. Vee, knowing that Geoffrey would get carried away by his performance, had every opportunity to leave the house after the show had started. There was plenty of time for her to have gone up to the Meckens'. Charlotte would have recognized her and let her in. A brief exchange, then Vee had taken Charlotte by surprise and strangled her. Put the body in the coal shed to delay its discovery and a brisk walk home to be back in time for the end of *I, Claudius*.

It was all conjecture, but it fitted. And, what was more, Charles thought he could prove it.

The proof lay on the table of his bedsitter. For reasons mainly of masochism (to see how much work other actors were getting), Charles always had the *Radio Times* delivered. Since he had no television and rarely listened to the radio, it was frequently thrown away unread. But on this occasion he felt sure it was going to be useful.

It was the Wednesday that interested him. He thought back to the Wednesday night when he had rung the Winters to get Robert Chubb's number. He remembered the time. Twenty-five to eleven, because he had looked at his watch after speaking to Kate Venables. And when he had spoken to Geoffrey Winter, there had been a break in their conversation while Vee was given advice on how to adjust the television for a good picture on BBC2.

Charles almost shouted out loud when the *Radio Times* confirmed his suspicions. At ten o'clock until ten-fifty on BBC2 on Wednesday night there had been a repeat of the Monday's episode of *I, Claudius*. Geoffrey Winter would not have been watching it, because he had missed so many of the earlier episodes.

So why should his wife watch the same programme for a second time in three days? Unless of course she hadn't been there to see it the first time.

Thirteen ...

CHARLES HAD CAUSE to be grateful to sour Reggie for forcing him into joining the Breckton Backstagers. As a Social Member, it was quite legitimate for him to be propping up the Back Room bar at a quarter past seven that evening.

There were not many faces he recognized. Robert Chubb gave him the sort of glance most people reserve for windows and a few others offered insincere half-smiles. The only person who greeted him with anything like conviviality was Denis Hobbs, who bought him a large Bell's. "You going to do some show or something down here then, Charles?"

Denis without Mary Hobbs was a refreshing change. He remained hearty, but didn't seem to have the same obligation to be raucously jovial which he had demonstrated on their previous meeting.

Charles denied that he was likely to break into amateur dramatics. "Just a handy bar." he explained, hoping that Denis wouldn't ask why it was handy for someone who lived fifteen miles away.

But Denis was a man without suspicion. He leaned forward to Charles and confided, "Exactly the reason I joined. I mean, you can't turn up the chance of a bar on your doorstep, can you?"

"So you don't act?"

Denis erupted with laughter. "Me? Bloody hell, I could no sooner act than have a baby. Blimey, me an actor—no, I'm a builder, that's what I am. Although Mary keeps trying to get me to say I work in the *construction industry*."

The mimicry which he put into the last two words suggested that he was not as devoid of acting talent as he had implied. "No, the acting bit's all Mary's. Very keen she is on all this arty-farty stuff. I tell you," he confided like a schoolboy with a dirty story, "I've been more bored in that theatre next door than a poof in a brothel. Still, Mary enjoys it. Keeps her out of my hair and keeps her off the streets, eh?" He laughed again robustly. "I'm only here for the beer—and I like to look at the scenery. The young female scenery, that is." He winked.

They were silent for a few moments. It wasn't an uncomfortable silence, just a pause of drinking companionship. Then, idly, to make conversation, Charles asked whether there had been any further developments on the burglary.

"No, not a thing. The police seem to think their best hope is to catch the villains when they try to get rid of the stuff. Apart from that, apparently there's not much chance. I mean, they've been all through the house and they haven't got any fingerprints or anything to go on."

"They left it very tidy?"

"Oh yes, everything put back, all the doors closed—very neat job."

"Nasty thing to happen, though."

"Yes. Still, we were insured, so it could have been worse. Mary was a bit cut up about what was taken, sentimental value, all that, but I went out and bought her a load more gear and that seems to have calmed her down a bit."

At that moment the Winters came in. Perhaps it was what Geoffrey had said in the morning, but they did look very together to Charles. As if they did share the complete relationship which he had described.

Denis Hobbs seemed to be slightly uneasy at their appearance, as if he suddenly had to be on his best behavior. Mary continually told him what a privilege it was to know such artistic luminaries as the Winters.

Geoffrey did a slight take, but greeted Charles cordially. As if by mutual agreement, they did not mention their earlier encounter.

Charles offered them drinks heartily. "What's it to be? I'm just taking advantage of my new membership."

Geoffrey wasn't fooled by that, but he made no comment. Charles wondered if the architect knew that he wanted to talk to Vee.

It was possible. Certainly Geoffrey seemed to be keeping his wife at his side to inhibit private conversations. A new thought struck Charles. Maybe Geoffrey had discovered his wife's crime and was set to defend her against investigation. That could make things difficult. Geoffrey's was a formidable mind to have in opposition.

But the architect's protection couldn't last long. The *Winter's Tale* rehearsal started at seven-thirty "and he gets furious if you're late, so I'd better go. Will you be going straight back home, Vee?"

The question was delivered with studied casualness, but Charles could sense the tension beneath it. Vee, either deliberately or not, didn't take the hint. "No, not straight away. I'll just buy Charles a drink. See you later. Hope it goes well."

"Fine." Geoffrey went through to the rehearsal room with a cheery wave. Or was it his impression of a cheery wave? Charles was getting paranoid about Geoffrey Winter's sincerity or lack of it.

He asked for a Bell's and Vee bought him a large one. Denis and a lot of the others round the bar had left and so, whether Geoffrey wanted it or not, Charles and Vee were alone together.

She commented on her husband's departure. "You know, he almost sounded as if he was jealous."

"What, of us?"

Vee shrugged. Charles laughed loudly, as if it was the best joke he had heard for a long time.

Interesting—straight away she put their meeting into a sexual context, just as she had done at the cast party. Once again he wasn't interested. And once again he felt she wasn't really interested either.

He decided that he would have to be a bit more subtle in questioning Vee than he had been with her husband. Better start at an uncontroversial level. "What are they rehearsing tonight?"

"Blocking the first two acts. So I'm not wanted."

"Oh, I didn't even realize you were in the production. What are you playing?"

"Perdita. Since yesterday." She pronounced it with triumph.

"You mean it was going to be . . . ?"

"Charlotte, yes. Of course, it's a terrible way to get a part, but it's an ill wind. . . ." Her regret was merely formal.

At least she wasn't disguising her satisfaction at Charlotte's removal from the scene. She was now back in her position as undisputed queen of the juve leads in the Breckton Backstagers. Charles would have thought she was a bit long in the tooth to be "the prettiest low-born lass that ever ran on the greensward" and a symbol of youthful beauty and regeneration, but now she was the best that Breckton had to offer. If she had killed Charlotte, then the returns were immediate.

Charles knew he had to play her gently. She was highly-strung and information would have to be wheedled out of her. He hoped Geoffrey had been discreet and not mentioned their meeting earlier in the day. He did not want her to be on her guard.

Starting with flattery seemed the best approach with someone as self-absorbed as she was. He asked her about her acting career at Breckton, regretting that he had never had the pleasure of seeing her in a production.

She needed no second invitation. He had in his time met a good few professional actors and actresses who assumed that everyone shared their own consuming interest in their theatrical doings, but never one as voluble as Vee Winter. Perhaps living with another king-size ego who also liked to talk about his acting, she didn't often get the chance to let rip in this way.

He got it all—the early aptitude for mimicry noted by loving parents, the success in elocution exams, the outstanding ability remarked upon by an English teacher, commendations at local festivals, the agonizing decision of the late teens as to whether to try for drama school and take it up professionally, then parental pressure and the final regrettable resolution to deprive the greater public of her talents.

At this point a pause was left for Charles to murmur some suitable insincerity about tragic waste.

"And then of course I married and decided that it would be wrong for me to do something that would take me away from Geoffrey for long periods of time. He is a complex character and can be a full-time job. I often think it's as well that we don't have children, because he needs so much of my attention that they might not get a look-in."

In this speech Charles could hear two threads of oft-repeated self-justification. First, the very common surburban housewife's explanation of why she never did anything more with her life, how the cares of marriage cut off in its bloom a career of unbelievable promise. In some cases—like, he reflected, that of Charlotte Mecken—it's true, but in most, where only moderate talent is involved, it's no more than a comforting fiction.

There was also the second well-rehearsed self-justification, for her childlessness. It was sad that this was

felt necessary, but there was a defensive quality to her
remarks about Geoffrey's demands on her time. Ironic to
Charles, with his knowledge of the other women among
whom Geoffrey spread those needs.

But she gave him a cue to find some purely practical
information. "You talk about Geoffrey being a full-time
job. Do you actually have a real one?"

"Job? Yes. I teach Speech and Drama at a local private
school."

"Oh."

This again seemed to need justification. "It's very close
and convenient. I get home for lunch. And of course I
think one can give a lot to young minds. If you've got an
enthusiasm for the theatre, it does communicate and
stimulate their interest."

"Oh, certainly."

"Also the little extra money comes in handy."

Knowing what he did about Geoffrey's business
affairs, Charles felt sure it did. He would imagine they
must have been living more or less exclusively on Vee's
income for some time. Perhaps Geoffrey even conducted
his affair with Charlotte on a grant from his wife.

But this digression on Vee's work did not divert her
long from the main subject of her dramatic triumphs. She
started to list the shows she had been in through a few
more drinks, and Charles's attention was wavering when
he suddenly heard himself being asked back to the house
to see some of her scrapbooks.

Instinctively he said yes, not certain whether scrapbooks were the latest form of etchings as a seduction bait.
The more time he could spend with Vee, the more relaxed
she became, the easier it was going to be to ask the
questions he wanted to.

It might also be useful to get inside the Winters' house
again. If Vee Winter did kill Charlotte, he was going to
need some tangible proof of it to convince the police.

Vee made their exit from the Back Room pointed, with
loud goodbyes to everyone and messages that she'd see

Geoffrey later. Again Charles felt the overtones of sexual
intrigue. Vee wanted to be seen leaving with him, possibly
to stimulate gossip among the Backbiters. But that was
all; she seemed to want the aura of an illicit liaison rather
than any illicit action. Or at least that was the impression
he got.

He would presumably find out if he was right when
they got back to the house.

As they walked back along the path to the main road,
Charles looked covertly at his companion. If she had
murdered Charlotte as he suspected, then this was the
route she must have taken on the Monday night. But her
face betrayed nothing.

The air was full of explosions and the sudden screams
of rockets. Of course, fireworks. November the Fifth. His
birthday. He recalled the old family joke that his mother
had been frightened into delivery by a wayward jumping
cracker.

On the common the celebrations were under way
round the huge bonfire. Presumably there had been an
effigy of Guy Fawkes hoisted on top of the pile, but now
all was consumed in the tall rippling flags of flame.

To one side of the bonfire, in a roped-off area, some
responsible fathers were donating Roman candles and
Catherine wheels. Charles knew that this was the new
approved policy; for greater safety, families were
encouraged to pool their fireworks into this kind of
communal party. To him it seemed to take away the
excitement and make the exercise rather pointless. Like
drinking non-alcoholic beer in motorway service cafés.

And in this case it didn't even seem to be particularly
safe. The leaping flames spat up lumps of burning debris,
some of which had landed in a nearby tree and kindled the
branches. The conflagration was in danger of getting out
of hand.

Still, there were lots of responsible fathers to deal with
the problem. Lots of over-insured men in their early

forties who no doubt drove Volvos with the side-lights on in the daytime. As Charles and Vee passed, there seemed to be an argument among them as to whether they should call the fire brigade or not.

To his amusement, Charles saw that the organizing spirit in the pro-fire brigade lobby was sour Reggie from the Backstagers. Taking his role as professional wet blanket literally this time. He scurried about issuing orders, followed by two small children of one sex or the other whose faces were as sour as their father's. It was strange to see the niggling committee man in another context.

Vee waved at Reggie, but he didn't see her. Once again she seemed to be drawing attention to her being with Charles, to set tongues wagging.

A group of overexcited children rushed towards them, involved in some inexplicable, but evidently very funny, game. Vee moved aside to let them pass. As she did so, the flames suddenly threw a spotlight on her face. The expression was one of infinite pain and bitterness.

They walked in silence down the paved path to the main road. There Vee stopped outside an off-licence. "No drink in the house, I'm afraid."

She selected a cheapish bottle of Italian red wine. Charles insisted on paying for it and she didn't argue. His new knowledge of the Winters' financial plight made sense of such details.

As Vee put her key in the front door, they heard the distant siren of a fire engine. Sour Reggie had triumphed. For the firework party-goers the evening's entertainment was ending.

But, as Vee Winter laid her arm on his shoulder and ushered him into the house, Charles Paris felt that perhaps his evening's entertainment was only beginning.

Fourteen . . .

CHARLES SIPPED HIS wine and tried not to look too downcast when Vee came in loaded with her theatrical memorabilia. Scrapbooks, programmes, a box of photographs and— most daunting of all—the cassette recorder that he had seen Geoffrey using. Oh dear, it looked as if he was going to get an Action Replay of her entire dramatic career.

He settled down to be bored out of his mind. Vee, he knew, was inflicting this on him because he was a professional actor. She wanted his commendation, she wanted him to say how improverished the British theatre had been by her decision to turn her back on it. Maybe she even wanted to gain his praise so that she would compare favorably with those whom he had condemned at the Critics' Circle.

He found her exhibitionism sad. The fact that she needed this bolstering. It showed that Geoffrey had too simple an interpretation of his wife's character. Her insecurity spoke in every nervous action. To think that she would not be jealous of another woman was totally wrong.

The overtones of sexuality which she gave to the proceedings also revealed her insecurity. She needed attention, she needed Charles to be aware that the two of them together was a potentially sexual scenario, but he felt that was all she needed. If he had made a pass at her, he would have got a considerate rebuff. She wouldn't have minded—in fact, she would rather have welcomed it as a boost to her ego and as something else to feel martyred about. She liked to think of herself as a tragic queen, resisting all blandishments from other men, because of her devotion to one man who was not really worthy of her.

Charles had not realized this vein of contempt which ran through Vee's feelings for her husband until the subject of children came up again. It was prompted by a photograph of Vee with another girl in Elizabethan dress who, apparently, had been a terribly good actress, but had given it all up when she started to have children. "Four I believe she's got now. Four. I suppose that could have been me, if things had turned out differently." She responded to Charles's quizzical look. "I mean, if I had married someone else."

"Oh," He sounded slightly embarrassed, as if he ought not to inquire further, knowing that this was the sure way to make her continue.

"Yes, with another man, no doubt I would be surrounded with the little brats, spending all my days at coffee parties and tea parties, talking about nappies and nursery schools." The edge she put into the words showed how much she was an outsider in the great incubator of Breckton. All the thoughts he'd had about Charlotte being ostracized by her childlessness applied even more strongly to Vee.

He continued his embarrassed act. "Well, er...I understood that nowadays there were things that could be done about infertility and...er...clinics and so on."

Vee smiled a martyred smile. "Maybe, but I don't think you'd ever get Geoffrey along to one of those. He couldn't admit to himself that . . . male pride in virility or . . . I'm sure you know all about that."

Again the remark was sexually loaded. Not quite a come-on, but a reminder that they were a man and woman alone together.

Charles thought quickly as he worked through the file of meaningless photographs. Vee's conviction that Geoffrey was to blame for their lack of family was obviously one of the supports of their marriage. She believed it, because it gave her superiority over him. She could watch with indulgence his philandering with other women, knowing his secret. And she was not afraid to divulge it.

Charlotte's pregnancy must have threatened the entire fabric of that illusion and Charlotte had had to be removed so that Vee could remain protected in her cocoon of fiction.

He knew he was right. All he needed was proof. It was time he got down to the details of his investigation.

In broaching the subject he was helped by the photographs There was a picture of Vee surrounded by adolescent youths in togas with laundry marks.

"Portia in *Julius Caesar* at school," she supplied.

"Ah, real *I, Claudius* stuff," he commented, grateful for the cue.

She laughed.

"Have you been watching it, Vee?" he asked casually.

"Oh yes. Seen every one. That was the big advantage of not doing *The Seagull*. Meant I could make it a regular date."

"Every Wednesday."

"No, I watch it on Mondays."

Charles took a risk. What he had to say next was going to sound more like interrogation than casual conversation. He hoped she wouldn't notice. "That's strange. I rang Geoffrey on Wednesday and I could have sworn he said you were watching it then."

He played it very light, but still threw her. She looked at him, flustered and bewildered. "Oh . . . oh yes, I did watch it on Wednesday this week."

He didn't volunteer any comment. Just left her to explain.

She did a good performance as someone sorting through her memory. "Oh, of course. My mother rang on Monday just after it had started. She always natters on so, the show was practically over by the time I got off the phone."

Charles joked, as if the information meant nothing to him, "I think everyone's mother's like that." But he felt sure she was lying.

"Yes, mine always rings at inconvenient times. Still, I suppose I shouldn't grumble, if the odd phone call keeps her happy. Better than continually traipsing up to Lytham St. Anne's to see her."

That was very helpful. He knew Vee's maiden name was le Carpentier. There shouldn't be too many old ladies of that name in Lytham St. Anne's with whom to check her alibi.

Eventually (and it seemed to take for ever) they came to the end of the photographs. "Fascinating," Charles lied.

Vee looked disappointed, as if she had expected more. What did she want him to do, for God's sake, say that she was the greatest actress to tread the boards on the evidence of a load of amateur snapshots?

But it seemed there was more evidence about to be offered. Vee was now turning her attention to the cassette player and the black plastic-covered box of cassettes. "Actually," she said with elaborate casualness, "I've got recordings here for some of the stuff I've done."

"Oh, really?" Charles gave the last dreg of his supply of simulated interest. "What, recorded off stage?"

"Some of them. Some I've just done at home—really just for my own benefit, so that I can get a kind of objective view of what I'm doing."

"I see."

"I thought you might like to hear one or two little bits.
It'd give you some idea of how I do act."

Charles quarried a smile from his petrifying features.
"Great." She fiddled with the machine. "Geoffrey lets you
borrow his recorder then?"

"It's not his, it's mine. He occasionally borrows it when
he's learning lines."

"And to dub off his music."

"What? Good God, no. He's far too much of a purist
for that. Only happy when music is being perfectly
reproduced on all that hi-fi stuff he's got upstairs. He
always says I'm a bit of a Philistine about it. I mean, I've
got some music cassettes—popular stuff—which I play
round the house, but he gets very sniffy about them. This
recorder's only mono for a start and he says you're
missing ninety per cent of the enjoyment if you don't hear
music in stereo."

"So he would never use it for music?"

"Not a chance. Look, there's a bit here that's an extract
from a production of *The Country Wife* that we did. I
played Mrs. Pinchwife. Got very good press. I think this
speech is quite amusing. Would you like to hear it?"

The affirmative smile was another triumph of engi-
neering.

Just before she switched it on, they both heard a
strange wail from outside. A sound like a child in pain.
Vee rose and Charles looked at her with some alarm.

"I must go to the kitchen to let him in," said Vee.

"Who is he?"

"Vanya."

"Vanya?"

"The cat."

As soon as she was out of the door, he leapt to the cassette
box. Her recorded voice wound on, but he didn't listen.
His mind was too full.

When he had first gone up to the study, Geoffrey

Winter had been copying Wagner's *Liebestod* from his expensive stereo on to this cheap mono cassette machine. Geoffrey had given some specious line about it being handier, which had seemed reasonable at the time, but which now seemed extremely suspicious.

If you don't want a cassette copy of a piece of music, then why copy it? Only one answer sprang to mind—in order to cover something already on the cassette.

He felt a prickle of excitement. Now at last he was on to something. Geoffrey's recording of the Wagner had taken place on the Tuesday, the day after Charlotte's murder. The architect must somehow have found out about his wife's crime and known that there was incriminating evidence on a cassette, which had to be removed. But Charles was due for supper just after he made the discovery, so he had to destroy the evidence while their guest was there without raising his suspicions. What was easier than to record over it?

Charles found the distinctive yellow and green container which held the cassette Geoffrey had used. There was a chance, a very long chance, that some part of its previous recording remained unerased. He slipped the thin rectangle into his pocket.

Meanwhile Vee Winter's interpretation of Wycherley ground on.

Suddenly the door opened and Geoffrey walked in. "Hello, Vee, I—"

The surprise was so great that even his well-controlled emotions were caught off their guard. In the flash of time before he recovered himself, Geoffrey's face bared his thoughts. He found another man alone in his house with his wife. And he was extremely suspicious.

Fifteen...

GERALD VENABLES WAS much more friendly when Charles rang him the next morning. Maybe he was less tired and the arrival of the weekend had cheered him. Or maybe the fact that it was the weekend meant he could relax his professional guard. Outside the office he could see Hugo's predicament as a case to be investigated rather than as an inconvenient and time-consuming legal challenge.

Whatever the cause, he agreed that they should meet and invited Charles down to Dulwich for lunch. As he signed off on the phone, he said. "So long, buster. See you at my joint round twelve. Okay, coochie-coo?" An encouraging sign.

As Charles walked from West Dulwich Station, he found that he was casting a Breckton eye over everything he saw, assessing the suburb from a suburban point of view. He hadn't quite got to the stage of pricing the houses he passed, but he could feel it wasn't far off.

Dulwich had the same air as Breckton of quiet desperation. Paranoid car-cleaning, wives pulled in every direction by children, buggies and shopping, determinedly jovial husbands taking the kids for a walk, track-suited executives sweating off some of the week's lunches in unconvinced jogging, others bearing their loads of wood and ceiling tiles from the brochured neatness of the Do-It-Yourself shop to the bad-tempered messes of a constructive weekend.

Gerald's house was predictably well-appointed. Part of a newish development, with that fraction more room between it and the next house which is the mark of success in the suburbs. The front door had a brass lion knocker and was white, with small square Georgian panels. The up-and-over garage door was panelled in the same way. In fact the whole scheme of the house was Georgian, with thin-framed white windows set in neat red brick. It was exactly the sort of house that anyone in Georgian England who happened to own two cars, a central heating oil tank, a television and a burglar alarm would have had.

Gerald was manifesting the schizophrenia of a Monday to Friday worker. He was dressed in a pale blue towelling shirt and evenly faded jeans (the summery image made possible by the blast of central heating which greeted Charles as he entered). His feet were encased in navy blue sailing shoes and a Snoopy medallion hung around his neck. This last was worn a bit self-consciously. Perhaps it was a fixture, always round the solicitorial neck beneath the beautifully-laundered cotton shirts and silk ties, but somehow Charles doubted it.

The shock of Gerald without a suit made him realize that it must have been nearly twenty years since he had seen his friend in informal gear. For a moment he wondered if he had come to the right house.

"Kate's taken the kids to some exhibition in Town, so we've got the place to ourselves. She sent love and so on. There's some kind of basic pâté lunch in the fridge for later. Have a beer?"

Predictably Löwenbräu. Charles descended into the depths of a light brown leather sofa and took a long swallow. "Well, are you beginning to think I might have a point?"

"Hardly, Charles, but I am willing to go through the evidence with you and see if there's anything. What do you reckon might have happened?"

Charles outlined his current view of Charlotte's death, moving swiftly from point to point. As he spoke, his conjectures took a more substantial form and he could feel an inexorable pull of logic.

Gerald was impressed, but sceptical. "I can see that that makes a kind of sense, but in a case like this you've got to have evidence. If you're ever going to convince the police that their nice neatly-sewn-up little case is not in fact nice and neatly-sewn-up at all, you're going to have to produce something pretty solid. All we've got so far is the slight oddness of a woman watching her favorite television programme twice in three days. And that could well be explained if it turns out that her story about her mother's phone call is true."

"I'd care to bet it isn't. Anyway, that's not all we have. We've also got this." With an actor's flourish Charles produced the yellow and green cassette box from his pocket.

"Oh yes." Gerald was not as overwhelmed by the gesture as he should have been. "You mentioned that. I'm afraid I don't quite see where you reckon that fits into the scheme of things."

"What, you don't want me to repeat all that business about my coming in and finding Geoffrey copying the Wagner?"

"No, I've got that. What I don't understand is what you are expecting to find on it. Except for Wagner. I mean, he could just have been copying it for a friend or something."

Charles wasn't going to shift from his proudly-achieved deduction. "No, I'm sure he was trying to hide something, to erase something."

"But what? What could possibly be put on tape that was incriminating? The average murderer doesn't record a confession just to make it easy for amateur detectives."

"Ha bloody ha. All right, I don't know what it is. I just know it's important. And the only way we're going to find out what's on it is by listening to the thing. Do you have a cassette player?"

"Of course," Gerald murmured, pained that the question should be thought necessary.

In fact he had a cassette deck incorporated into the small city of matt grey Bang and Olufsen hi-fi equipment that spread over the dark wooden wall unit. The speakers stood on the floor like space age mushrooms.

"Now I reckon," said Charles as Gerald fiddled with the console, "our best hope is that there's something right at the beginning, that he started recording too far in and didn't wipe all the—"

The opening of the *Prelude* from Wagner's *Tristan und Isolde* gave him the lie.

"Well, if that was our best hope. . . ." Gerald observed infuriatingly, as he bent to fiddle with more knobs.

When he was happy with the sound, he sat down with a smug smile on his face, waiting to be proved right. The *Prelude* wound moodily on. Charles remembered how cheap he had always found the emotionalism of Wagner's outpourings. He began to get very bored.

After about five minutes it became clear that Gerald was going through the same process of mental asphyxiation. "Charles, can't we switch it off? Kate's taken me to this stuff, but I've never cared for it much."

"No. Some American once said Wagner's music is better than it sounds."

"It needs to be. I think it's going to go on like this for some time and we're not going to get any dramatic murder confessions."

"I agree. Let's spool through. There might be something where he changed sides. That's a C90 cassette, forty-five minutes each way. The LP could only have had about twenty minutes each side, so he must have flipped the disc. Might be something there."

There wasn't. They could hear the blip of the pick-up being lifted off, then the slight hiss of erased tape until the bump of the stylus back on the other side, the tick of the homing grooves and the return of the music.

"No." Gerald's smugness was increasing.

"Let's try the end. Yes, if there's only forty minutes on the disc and it's a forty five minute tape. . . ." Charles felt a new surge of excitement at the thought.

He tensed as Gerald spooled through till nearly the end of the tape and uttered a silent prayer as the replay button was pressed.

God was apparently deaf. Tape hiss. Again, nothing but tape hiss. "I think he just left the Record button down and let the tape run through until it was all erased."

"Yes, I suppose so," Charles agreed gloomily. Then, with sudden memory—"No, but he didn't. I was there. I remember quite distinctly. Perhaps he had intended to do that, but because I was there he switched it off when the music stopped. He must have erased the last bit after that. Which would suggest to me that he did have something important to hide." Suddenly he got excited. "Look, suppose he missed a bit just at the end of the music. . . ."

"Why should he?"

"Well, with some of these cheap cassette players it's difficult to press the Play button and Record at exactly the same time. He might have put down the Play a moment earlier and left something unerased."

"But surely he would have heard anything and gone back over it."

"Not necessarily. Most of these machines have another button with which you switch off the sound to prevent microphone howlround. So he wouldn't have heard it. And, given his great respect for music, even in this situation I don't think he'd want to risk going back and wiping the final reverberation of his Wagner."

"It sounds pretty unlikely to me."

"It is. But it's possible. Spool back to the end of the music."

With the expression of someone humoring the mentally infirm, the solicitor returned the controls. It was the end of the *Liebestod*. The soprano warbled to death and the orchestra rose to its sullen climax. The regular hiss of the stylus on the center groove seemed interminable. Then abruptly it was lifted off. This sound was followed by the woolly click of the recorder being switched off. Then another click as it had been restarted and, seconds later, a third as the Record button had been engaged.

Between the last two clicks there was speech.

Charles and Gerald looked at each other as if to confirm that they had both heard it. They were silent; the evidence was so fragile, it could suddenly be blown away.

Charles found his voice first. "Spool back. Play it again," he murmured huskily.

Again Wagner mourned in. Again the pick-up worried against the center of the record. Then the clicks. And, sandwiched between them, Geoffrey Winter's voice. Saying two words—no, not so much—two halves of two words.

"-ed coal-" Charles repeated reverentially. "Play it again."

Gerald did so. "It's cut in the middle of some word ending in *ed*, and it sounds as though the *coal* is only the beginning of a word too."

"What words begin with *coal?*"

Charles looked straight at Gerald. "*Coal shed*, for one."

"Good God." For the first time the lines of scepticism left the solicitor's face. "And what about words ending in *ed*? There must be thousands."

"Thousands that are spelled that way, not so many that are pronounced like that."

"No. I suppose there's *coal shed* again. If the two parts came the other way around . . . ?"

"Or there's *dead*, Gerald."

"Yes," the solicitor replied slowly. "Yes, there is."

"May I use your phone, Gerald?"

"What for?"

"I'm going to crack Vee Winter's alibi."

"Oh."

"Don't sound so grumpy about it. Cheapest time to phone your friends—after six and at weekends. I'll pay for the call, if you like."

"No, it's not that. The firm sees to the phone bill anyway."

"Of course. I'd forgotten. You never use your own money for anything, do you?"

"Not if I can help it." Gerald smiled complacently.

Given Lytham St. Anne's and the unusaul name of le Carpentier, Directory Inquiries had no difficulty in producing Vee's mother's phone number. Charles put his finger down on the bar of Gerald's Trimphone and prepared to dial.

"Are you just going to ask her direct, Charles? Won't she think it's a bit odd?"

"I'm not going to ask her direct. I have a little plan worked out, which involves using another voice. Don't worry."

"But that's illegal," wailed Gerald as Charles dialled. "You can't make illegal calls on a solicitor's telephone."

Mrs. le Carpentier answered the phone with the promptness of a lonely old lady.

"Hello. Telephone Engineer." Charles was pleased with the voice. He had first used it in a stillborn experimental play called *Next Boat In* (Captured all the bleakness and, I'm afraid, all the tedium of dockland"— *Lancashire Evening News*). He thought it was a nice touch to be Liverpudlian for Lytham St. Anne's.

"Oh, what can I do for you? I hope there's nothing wrong with the phone. I'm an old lady living on my own and—"

The Telephone Engineer cut in reassuringly over Mrs. le Carpentier's genteel tones. "No, nothing to worry about. Just checking something. We had a complaint—somebody reported that your phone was continually engaged when they tried to ring, so I just have to check that the apparatus was in fact in a state of usage during the relevant period."

"Ah, I wonder who it could have been. Do you know who reported the fault?"

"No, Madam."

"It could have been Winnie actually. She lives in Blundellsands. We play bridge quite often and it's possible she was trying to set up a four for—"

The Telephone Engineer decided he didn't want to hear all of Mrs. le Carpentier's social life. "Yes, Madam. I wonder if we could just check the relevant period. The fault was reported last Monday. Apparently someone tried to call three times between nine and half past in the evening. Was the apparatus being used at this time?"

So confident was he of a negative response that her reply threw him for a moment. "I beg your pardon, Madam?"

"Yes, it was in use."

"Oh. Oh." Still, it wasn't necessarily Vee to whom she was speaking. "Local calls, were they, Madam?"

"Oh no, it was just one call. Long distance."

"Where to? We have to check, Madam, when it's been reported."

"It was a call to Breckton. That's in Surrey. Near London."

Charles felt the concoction of logic he had compounded trickling away from him. "Are you absolutely confident that that was the time, Madam?"

"Absolutely. It was the time that that *I, Claudius* was on the television."

"Oh."

"Yes, you see, I saw it for the first time last week and I

thought it was a shocking programme. So much violence and immorality. My daughter had mentioned that she watched it, but after I'd seen what it was all about, I thought it was my duty as a mother to ring her up while it was on, so that she couldn't watch it. Do you see?"

"I see," Charles replied dully. Yes, he saw. He saw all his ideas suddenly discredited, he saw that he must flush every thought he'd ever had about the case out of his mind and start again with nothing.

Mrs. le Carpentier was still in righteous spate. "I think too many parents nowadays neglect their duties as their children's moral guardians. I mean, Victoria's over thirty, but she still needs looking after. She mixes with all kinds of theatrical people and—"

"Victoria?"

"My daughter."

"Good God."

"That's another thing I don't like in young people today—taking the name of the Lord in vain. It's—"

"Mrs. le Carpentier, thank you very much. You've been most helpful. I can confirm that there is nothing wrong with your apparatus."

"Oh good. And do you think maybe I should ring Winnie?"

"Yes, I would."

He slumped on to the sofa, not hearing Gerald's remonstrances about the illegality of impersonating people over the telephone and the number of laws under which this action could be charged and how the fact that the owner did not stop the crime might well make him an accessory.

It all flowed past Charles. The void which had been left in his mind by the confirmation of Vee's alibi had only been there for a few seconds before new thoughts started to flood in. He pieced them together into a rough outline and then spoke, shutting Gerald up with a gesture.

"Vee's real name is Victoria."

"So what? What about her alibi? Was she telling the truth?"

"Oh yes." Charles dismissed the subject.

"Well then, that seems to put the kybosh on the whole—"

"But don't you see—her real name is Victoria."

"Yes, but—"

"I should have guessed. The way all these amateur actors fiddle about with their names, it should have been obvious."

"I don't see that her name is important when—"

"It is important, Gerald, because it means that it was Vee whom Charlotte was going to see at one o'clock the day after she was murdered. During the school lunch hour. Charlotte couldn't stand all those affected stage names, so she would have called her Victoria as a matter of principle. And I bet that the reason she was going to see Vee was to tell her she was pregnant."

"So Vee didn't already know?"

"No."

"But surely that throws out all your motivation for her to have done the murder and—"

"She didn't do the murder. Forget Vee. She doesn't have anything to do with it."

"Then who did kill Charlotte?"

"Geoffrey Winter."

"But Geoffrey didn't have any motivation to kill her. He had a very good affair going, everything was okay."

"Except that Charlotte was pregnant."

"We don't even know that."

"I'll bet the police post mortem showed that she was. Go on, you can ask them when you're next speaking."

"All right, let's put that on one side for the moment and proceed with your wild theorizing." The lines of scepticism were once again playing around Gerald's mouth.

"Geoffrey and Vee Winter are a very close couple. In spite of his philandering, he is, as he told me, very loyal to her. Now all marriages are built up on certain myths and the myth which sustains Vee is that her childlessness is Geoffrey's fault. His infertility gives her power. She can tolerate his affairs, secure in the knowledge that he will come back to her every time. But if it were suddenly proved that in fact he could father a child, everything on which she had based their years together would be taken away from her. I think, under those circumstances, someone as highly-strung as she is could just crack up completely.

"Geoffrey knew how much it would mean to her, so when Charlotte told him she was pregnant, he had to keep that knowledge from his wife. No doubt his first reaction was to try to get her to have an abortion, but Charlotte, nice little Catholic girl that she was, would never have consented to that. Equally, being a conventional girl, she would want to have the whole thing open, she'd want to talk to his wife, even maybe see if Vee would be prepared to give Geoffrey up.

"So she rang Vee up and fixed to meet her on the Tuesday during her lunch hour. On the Monday she went up to Villiers Street for her assignation with Geoffrey and told him what she intended to do. He could not allow the confrontation of the two women to take place. He decided that Charlotte must never go and see Vee. So he killed her."

Charles leaned back with some satisfaction. The new theory felt much more solid than the old one. It left less details unaccounted for.

Gerald said exactly what Charles knew he would. "I'm impressed by the psychological reasoning, Charles, but there is one small snag. Geoffrey Winter had an alibi for the only time he could have murdered Charlotte. He was at home rehearsing his lines so loudly that his next door neighbor complained to the police. How do you get round that one?"

Gerald couldn't have set it up more perfectly for him if he had tried. "This is how he did it." Charles picked the cassette box up off the table.

"So easy. He even told me he used the cassette recorder for learning his lines. All he had to do was to record a full forty-five minutes of *The Winter's Tale* on to this cassette, put it on, slip out of the French windows of his study, go and commit the murder, come back, change from recording to his own voice and insure that he started ranting loudly enough to annoy his neighbor with whom his relationship was already dodgy. After previous disagreements about noise, he felt fairly confident that she would call the police, thus putting the final seal on his watertight alibi."

Gerald was drawn to this solution, but he was not wholly won over. "Hmm. It seems that one has to take some enormous imaginative leaps to work that out. I'd rather have a bit more evidence."

"We've got the cassette. And I've suddenly realized what it means. The words—it's Leontes."

"It's what?"

"Leontes in *The Winter's Tale*. One of the most famous lines in the play. When he speaks of Hermione's eyes, he says; 'Stars, stars! And all eyes else *dead coals*.' That's the bit we've got on the tape."

Gerald was silent. Then slowly, unwillingly, he admitted, "Do you know, you could be right."

"Of course I'm right," said Charles. "Now where's that lunch you were talking about?"

Sixteen...

CHARLES DIDN'T WANT to hurry things. He was now confident that he knew how Charlotte had been killed, and he could afford to take time to check it. There was no point in confronting Geoffrey Winter or going to the police with an incompletely researched solution.

He left Gerald late on the Saturday afternoon. (Gerald wanted to watch *Doctor Who* and Charles didn't really much.) They agreed that Charles should make various further investigations and then report back. Gerald was now more or less convinced by the new solution, but his legal caution remained.

Since there was nothing useful he could do that day, Charles went for the evening to one of his old haunts, the Montrose, a little drinking club round the back of the Haymarket. As he expected, it was full of out-of-work actors (and even, after the theatres finished, some in-work ones). A great deal of alcohol was consumed.

He woke feeling pretty ropey on the Sunday morning and did the tube and train journey to Breckton on automatic

pilot. It was only when he emerged into the stark
November sunlight outside the suburban station that
consciousness began to return.

Blearily he reminded himself of the plan he had vaguely
formed the day before. He had come down to Breckton to
check the timing of the crime, to retrace the steps that
Geoffrey Winter had taken on the Monday night and see
if it was feasible for him to have killed Charlotte in the
forty-five minutes the tape allowed.

Charles was early. Since he didn't want to run the risk
of meeting any of the principals in the crime, he had
decided to conduct his exploration after two-thirty when
they would all be emoting over *The Winter's Tale* up at
the Backstagers.

He arrived just after twelve, which was a remarkably
convenient time for him to go into a pub and kill time and
his hangover at one blow.

There was a dingy little Railway Tavern adjacent to the
station which was ideal for his purposes. The railway line
was at some distance from the posher residential side of
Breckton and he was in no danger of meeting any of the
Backstagers down there.

When he entered the pub, it was clear that the clientéle
came from "the other side of the railway," an expression
of subtle snobbery that he had heard more than once from
the theatrical circle. On the "other side of the railway"
there was a council estate, yet another socio-geological
stratum in the complex structure of Breckton. At the
bottom was the bedrock of "the other side of the railway
line," then the unstable mixture of rising lower middle
and impoverished upper middle class "the other side of
the main road" (where Geoffrey and Vee lived), then the
rich clay of the newer detached executive houses like the
Meckens' and finally the lush topsoil of extreme affluence
which manifested itself in mock-Tudor piles like the
Hobbses'. Across the strata ran the faults and fissures of
class and educational snobbery as well, so that a full
understanding of the society would be a lifetime's study.

Charles ordered a pint which made his brain blossom out of its dessication like a Japanese flower dropped in water.

Being a Sunday, there was nothing to eat in the pub except for a few cheese biscuits and cocktail onions on the bar, but Charles was quite happy to resign himself to a liquid lunch.

As he sat and drank, his mind returned to Charlotte's murder. Not in a depressed or panicky way, but with a kind of intellectual calm. He felt as he had sometimes done when writing a play, the comforting assurance that he'd sorted out a satisfactory plot outline and only needed to fill in the details.

And little details were slotting into his scenario of the death of Charlotte Mecken. One was disturbing. He was beginning to think that Geoffrey might be on to his suspicions.

First, the interrogation in his office must have put him on his guard, if Charles's phone call on the evening of Hugo's arrest hadn't already done so. But there was something else. On the Friday night, when Geoffrey had discovered Charles in his sitting room, he had looked extremely suspicious. At the time, Charles had assumed that the suspicion had a sexual basis.

But, as he thought back over the circumstances, he found another interpretation. When Geoffrey arrived, the cassette player was running, reproducing Vee's performance of Wycherley's Mrs. Pinchwife. Geoffrey had entered speaking to Vee, as if he expected her to be in the room. Maybe the suspicion arose when he saw that he had been fooled by the sound of the cassette player, that in fact he had been caught by his own deception. If that were the case, then he might have thought that Charles was further advanced in his investigations than he was and that playing the tape of Vee had been a deliberate set-up to see how the supposed murderer would react.

It was quite a thought. Geoffrey was a cold-blooded killer and if he could dispose of his mistress without a qualm, he would have little hesitation in getting rid of anyone else who stood in his way. Charles would have to tread warily.

Because if Geoffrey Winter did try to kill him, he would do the job well. He was a meticulous planner. Charles thought of the set model for *The Caucasian Chalk Circle* in Geoffrey's study. Every move carefully considered. Little plastic people being manipulated, disposed (and disposed of) according to the director's will.

The thought of danger cast a chill over the conviviality of the pub and the glow of the fourth pint. Well, the solution was to get to the source of the danger as soon as possible, to prove Geoffrey's guilt and have him put away before he could make a hostile move.

The pub was closing. Charles went to the Gents with the uncomfortable feeling that the amount he had consumed and the cold weather were going to make him want to go again before too long.

It was after two-thirty when he reached the Winters' road. He walked along it at an even pace, apparently giving their house no deeper scrutiny than the others. Somehow he felt that the watchers of Breckton were still alert behind their net curtains on Sunday afternoons.

The Winters themselves had resisted the suburban uniform of net curtains, so from a casual glance he could feel pretty confident that they were out. But he did not start his timed walk from then. He felt sure there must be a route from the back of the house.

When he got to the end of the road, his hunch was proved right. The gardens of the row of identical semis (identical to everyone except their proud owners) backed on to the gardens of the parrallel row in the next road. Between them ran a narrow passage flanked with back gates into minute gardens.

The alley was concreted over, its surface cracked and brown, marked with moss and weeds. Suburban secrecy insured that the end fencing of all the gardens was too high for anyone walking along the alley to see in (or, incidentally, to be seen).

As Charles walked along, he could hear sounds from the gardens. The scrape of a trowel, a snatch of conversation, the sudden wail of a child, very close the snuffling bark of a dog. But except for the occasional flash of movement through the slats of fencing, he saw no one.

And this was in the middle of Sunday afternoon. After dark one could feel absolutely secure in passing unseen along the alley. And Geoffrey Winter must have known that.

When he reached the Winter's garden gate, he pressed close to the fence and squinted through a chink. He could see the distinctive wall-coloring of Geoffrey's study and, outside it, the little balcony and staircase, so convenient for anyone who wanted to leave the room unnoticed after dark.

As anticipated, the pressure on his bladder was becoming uncomfortable and he stopped to relieve himself where he stood. He was again struck by the secluded nature of the alley, which enabled him to behave impolitely in such a polite setting.

Then he started his timed walk. He reckoned Geoffrey must have allowed a maximum of forty minutes. *I, Claudius* lasted fifty, but he could only get forty-five minutes of *The Winter's Tale* on one side of the tape. Five minutes would be a buffer to allow for the unexpected.

Charles set off at a brisk walk. If Geoffrey had run, the timing would have been different, but Charles thought that was unlikely. A man running after dark attracts attention, while a man walking passes unnoticed.

The alley behind the houses came out on to the main road exactly opposite the footpath up to the common. There was a "No Cycling" notice at the entrance. The path was paved until it opened out on to the common.

It was the first time Charles had seen this open expanse

in daylight. In the center were a couple of football pitches, which were reasonably well maintained, but the fringes of the common were ill-tended and untidy and had been used as a dumping ground by the nice people of Breckton. Superannuated fridges and rusty buckets looked almost dignified beside the more modern detritus of garish plastic and shredded polythene. It was an eyesore, the sort of mess about which aggrieved rateplayers no doubt wrote righteous letters to the local paper. To Charles it seemed a necessary part of the suburban scene, the secret vice which made the outward rectitude supportable.

The half-burnt crater of the bonfire doused by the fire brigade at sour Reggie's behest gave the dumping ground an even untidier and more melancholy appearance.

The bonfire had been built where the footpath divided into two. The right-hand fork went up towards the Backstagers' club-rooms and the Hobbses' house. Charles took the other path which led towards the Meckens'.

He was feeling the need for another pee, but resolutely hung on, because any unscheduled stop would ruin his timing. He wished he had got a stopwatch, so that he could suspend time long enough to make himself comfortable. But he hadn't.

Even on a Sunday afternoon there were not many people up on the common. A few bored fathers trying to feign interest in their toddlers, one or two pensioners pretending they had somewhere to go. Breckton boasted other, more attractive parklands, equipped with such delights as swings and duck-ponds, and most of the inhabitants went there for their exercise.

It had rained during the week, but the path had dried out and was firm underfoot as Charles continued his brisk stroll. When he got to the other side of the common, the footpath once again had a proper surface of dark tarmac. His desert boot soles sounded dully as he trod.

To maintain his excitement he made a point of not looking at his watch until the journey was complete. He didn't stop when he got to Hugo's house. His memories of the net curtain snooper made him unwilling to draw attention to himself.

When he had gone one house-length beyond (which he reckoned would allow for going over the gravel drive to the front door), he looked at his watch.

Sixteen minutes. Geoffrey, with his longer stride, might have done it in fifteen. Say the same time each way. That gave eight or ten minutes in the house. Charlotte would have recognized him and let him in immediately, so there would have been no delay.

And eight or ten minutes was plenty of time for a determined man to strangle a woman.

If, of course, the murder weapon was to hand. On that kind of schedule, Geoffrey couldn't afford time to look for a scarf. He must have known where it was or . . . no, there was something missing there.

Charles tried to focus his mind on the problem. He summoned up the image of Charlotte in the coal shed, surprised untidily by the torch beam. He remembered her face. The red hair that framed it had looked unnatural, as if it were dyed, against the horrible greyness of her flesh. And that thin knotted Indian print scarf which couldn't hide the trickle of dried blood and the purply-brown bruises on her neck. Bruises almost like love-bites. He remembered what he had thought at the time, how she had looked so young, embarrassingly unsophisticated, like a teenager with a scarf inadequately hiding the evidence of a heavy petting session.

Good God—maybe that's what it had been. After all, she had seen Geoffrey at lunchtime. By then he must have planned the murder. It would be typical of the man's mind if he had deliberately marked her neck, knowing that, respectable married women that she was, she would be bound to put on a scarf to cover the bruising.

Then Geoffrey could go round in the evening,

confident that the murder weapon would be to hand. Under those circumstances, he did not have to leave long for the strangling.

Charles shivered as he thought of the cold-bloodedness with which the crime had been planned.

He felt like an athlete in training for a major event. Everything was moving towards a confrontation with Geoffrey Winter. It was going to be risky to confront the villain with what he had deduced, but he couldn't see any way round it. The evidence he had was minimal and certainly not enough to persuade the police to change their tack. So his only hope was to elicit some admission of guilt from Geoffrey.

The fear of the man was building inside Charles. He felt increasingly certain that Geoffrey had read his suspicions and he wanted to keep the advantage by going to see his adversary rather than waiting for his adversary to search him out.

Within the next twenty-four hours, Charles knew, something conclusive was going to happen.

He went back to Hereford Road on the Sunday evening and rang Sally Radford. He had the sensation of a condemned man deserving a final treat.

But he didn't get his treat. Sally was glad to hear from him, but, sorry, she'd got a friend coming round that evening. Yes, maybe another time.

It shouldn't have hurt him. They'd agreed no strings, but it did cause a pang. The idea of a completely casual encounter with no obligations had always appealed to him, but now it had happened he was full of the need to establish continuity, to keep it going, to make something of it.

When he'd rung off from Sally, he contemplated ringing Frances, but procrastinated once again. He wrote off the idea of female company for the evening and went back to the Montrose. If he could keep on topping up his alcohol level, he might retain his mood of confidence and face the ordeal ahead without too much introspection.

Seventeen...

IN SPITE OF the knowledge of inevitable confrontation, Charles still had a career to pursue. Whatever the outcome of his meeting with Geoffrey Winter, he was still meant to be recording the second batch of Bland radio commercials on the Tuesday morning. The events of the week had pushed that from his mind.

It was only when he thought about it on the Monday morning that he realized he had better check the details. After all, it was Hugo Mecken's campaign and Hugo would not be able to conduct it from the remand wing of Brixton Prison.

He rang through to Mills Brown Mazzini and asked for Ian Compton. It turned out to be the right choice. Ian told him with no little complacency that he had taken over the Bland account. Charles wondered how much more of Hugo's authority the young wheeler-dealer had managed to annex since the Creative Director had been off the scene.

"I was just ringing to check that tomorrow's still on as

per arrangement. Eleven o'clock at the same studio for the rest of the radios."

"Yes, I should think that'll stand, though there's a slight question mark over it. May need some time for reworking of the copy. I'm having a meeting with Farrow this afternoon. Won't really know for sure till after that. Can I ring you in the morning?"

"Not quite sure of my movements."

"You should be. Got to always be on call in the voice-over business."

Charles ignored the young man's patronizing tone. "I'll ring you. Either at the office in the morning or—have you a home number where I can get you this evening?"

"Won't be in. Got a film dubbing session at Spectrum Studios."

"For the Bland campaign?" Charles pricked up his ears. Was Ian Compton getting some other voice-over work done on Bland behind his back?

"No, no. It's a private film production I'm working on. Doing a session with Diccon, just dubbing the voice."

"Oh, I see." It was hard to know whether to believe it or not. Ian Compton wouldn't hesitate to lie if it served his ends. On the other hand, he did work on a lot of other projects apart from Bland. "How is Diccon?"

"Oh, he's in a pretty lousy mood at the moment."

"What, not getting work?"

"You must be joking. That cookie is one of the busiest voices in the business. Clears twenty grand a year easy. No, he seems very cut up about Hugo's wife. I think he had quite a thing for her."

"She was a very nice lady."

"So I hear. It seems everyone thought so except Hugo." Ian did not attempt to disguise the note of triumph in his voice. He was giving a reminder that Hugo Mecken was no longer a challenge to the bright young whiz-kid of Mills Brown Mazzini.

Charles decided that the confrontation should take place in Geoffrey's office. It would be quiet, no danger of interruptions. He told Gerald what he was going to do. Gerald disapproved, but Charles wanted someone to know in case he didn't return from the interview.

It was about a quarter to eleven on the Monday morning when he entered the building in Villiers Street. He mounted the stairs with one part of his mind immobilized by fright and the other irreverently providing sound track music and offering Sydney Carton's dramatic lines for use when mounting scaffolds to the sneers of unruly mobs.

All of which build-up was somewhat wasted when he found the door of Geoffrey Winter Associates firmly locked.

There was no light on inside. His mind, still running on romantic rails, summoned up the image of Geoffrey Winter sprawled over his desk, the smoking revolver clutched in his hand, his brains spattered on the wall behind. The villain who knew he had been found out and who had done the decent thing.

Wisely recognizing that this image was a little fanciful, he started knocking on the door to attract attention. A light tap produced nothing from inside, so he tried a more robust blow and then heavy hammering.

The last did raise a reaction, but it came from the floor below. An aggrieved young man with elastic bands holding up his shirt sleeves came and complained. So far as he knew, Mr. Winter wasn't in. He hadn't heard him coming up the stairs that morning. And surely the fact that there had been no reply to "that bloody awful din you're making" indicated that there was nobody in the office.

Charles apologized and left the building. But he was too keyed up to drop it there. He had steeled himself to a meeting with Geoffrey Winter that day and somehow he had to arrange it.

He went into Charing Cross Station and rang the Winters' number from a call-box.

Vee answered. That in itself was strange. If she was a teacher, she should surely be in class at that time. Also she sounded even tenser and more emotional than usual. She had snatched up the phone on the first ring.

"Could I speak to Geoffrey, please? It's Charles Paris."

"No, I'm sorry, he's not here." She sounded near to tears.

"Do you know when he's likely to be back? I've been to his office and I couldn't find him there."

"No, I've no idea. He's. . . ." She stopped, leaving the word dramatically in the air. Charles was conscious of her acting instincts vying with genuine emotion.

"Is he likely to be in this evening? Do you know?"

"No, I don't. I—" Again she cut short, uncertain whether to confide more. Charles felt a new panic. Had Geoffrey done a bunk?

But Vee could not keep her secrets to herself. In the same way that she had confided Geoffrey's supposed infertility to Charles, she couldn't resist the dramatic and martyring implications of her latest piece of news. "Oh, what the hell. I might as well tell you. The whole country will no doubt know soon enough. Geoffrey's been arrested."

"Arrested?"

"Yes, the police came round this morning before he left for work."

Charles murmured some suitable words about how sorry he was and how sure he was that it would soon all be cleared up and how it must all be a ghastly mistake, but he had stopped thinking what he was saying. He concluded the conversation and then walked slowly, numbly, down to the Embankment.

He looked into the murky, swirling Thames. He tried to tell himself all kinds of other things, but ultimately he couldn't deny that he felt profoundly disappointed.

So that was it. The police must have been following his investigations in exact parallel. They must have worked out in just the same way how Geoffrey had contrived his alibi and managed to leave his room for the vital forty minutes.

Or no, perhaps he was flattering himself. The police had probably far outstripped his feeble investigations. They must have done. They wouldn't make an arrest without convincing evidence. He felt diminished and unnecessary.

He tried to argue himself out of this selfish mood. After all, what did it matter who had found the truth, so long as it had been revealed? Hugo could now go free, that was the main thing.

It didn't help. Depressingly he thought how little Hugo cared whether he was free or not. The release might well be a licence for him to commit suicide or, more slowly, drink himself to death.

Still, right had triumphed. He tried to feel glad about it.

With an effort he drew himself away from the river and started back to the station. Better ring Gerald and bring him up to date. Though if charges against his client were about to be dropped, he'd probably know already.

He didn't. He reacted strongly when Charles told him. But the reaction was not that of Gerald Venables the amateur sleuth; it was all solicitor. This new development changed circumstances for his client. He would get on to the Breckton police immediately.

"Okay," said Charles dismally. "Well, I'm going back to Hereford Road. So if there's any interesting development, just let me know."

But he didn't really think any new development would concern him. He felt excluded, the one boy in the class without a party invitation.

He bought a new bottle of Bell's on the way back to Hereford Road. He was going to drink himself into a stupor. After the tension of the last week, this sudden anti-climax had let him down like a punctured air-bed.

The phone was ringing when he entered the house. He ran up to the landing and picked it up.

It was Gerald. Very cross. "Are you trying to make me look like a complete fool? I've just spoken to the Superintendent at Breckton. He must think I'm a bloody lunatic. And you're not the most popular person down at the station either.

"Geoffrey Winter has been arrested, yes. But it has nothing to do with the Mecken murder at all. He's been arrested for stealing some jewellery from a couple called Hobbs."

"Oh my God." Charles saw the bottom card being withdrawn from the great edifice he had built up.

"So you were right, Charles. Geoffrey Winter did have something to hide about what he was doing last Monday night. But it wasn't what your fertile imagination gave him to do."

"But—"

"And what's more—just for your information—I've heard about the post mortem. Charlotte Mecken was not pregnant."

Eighteen...

LIKE THE CAT in a Tom and Jerry cartoon, Charles Paris continued running after the ground had crumbled away beneath his feet, before the inevitable realization and the windmill-armed plummeting descent to the depths.

Geoffrey Winter must be guilty of Charlotte's murder. All the motivation fitted; Charles couldn't start again the laborious reconstruction of emotion and opportunity with another subject. He refused to accept it.

But like the cat, he became increasingly aware that he was running on air. Whichever way he worked it, Geoffrey could not have committed both crimes on the Monday evening.

Unwilling to relinquish his theory, Charles went down to Breckton to time it all out again. He felt none of the elation of the previous day; as time passed he saw his logic falling apart.

He tried the trip from the Winters' house to the

Meckens' via the Hobbses', he tried it the other way round, going to the Meckens' first, but there was just not enough time for anyone to have committed the two crimes.

Visiting the two houses added another five minutes to the round trip. Which left five or less for murder. Which was cutting it fine by the standards of the most experienced assassin. He tried adding the extra five minutes which he had reckoned Geoffrey would have left as a safety margin, but the sums still seemed pretty unlikely.

They seemed even unlikelier when he remembered that he had not allowed any time for the actual theft from the Hobbses' house. He had only timed the round trip of going past the house. If that were all that had been involved, the murder might have been possible. But even if Geoffrey knew the house well and knew exactly where Mary Hobbs kept her jewellery, it was still going to take him some time to break in, get through the house in the dark armed only with a torch and grab the loot. The absolute minimum was four minutes. In fact, considering the care with which Geoffrey had covered his tracks, it must have been six or eight.

Which left very little time to murder Charlotte Mecken.

Charles sat down on a bench on the common as it started to get dark. He was furious. There was no way it would work.

It wasn't just the timing. If Charlotte hadn't been pregnant, then none of his complex sequence of motivation worked either.

Depression took over. So everything was as obvious as it seemed. Hugo Mecken had killed his wife and Geoffrey Winter, in desperate financial straits because of his failing architect's business, had stolen some jewellery from the richest people he knew. The fact that the two incidents had taken place on the same evening had been mere coincidence.

The new turn of events changed his opinion of Geoffrey. While he had thought of the architect as Charlotte's murderer, he had had a kind of respect for him, for the cold-blooded intellect that could plan such a crime. But now he knew that all that planning had been for a petty theft, a mean robbery from some supposed friends.

And Geoffrey's was not a great intellect. He had shown remarkable ineptitude in the execution of his crime, however clever the original conception of the cassette alibi. For a start, there had been his confused exit from the Hobbses' house when he saw Robert Chubb pass. Leaving his torch behind on the window sill was the real mark of the amateur.

The way he had been caught had been equally incompetent. Charles had heard it all from Gerald. The thief had gone along the jewellers' stands in the Portobello Road on the Saturday morning trying to sell his loot. One of the dealers had bought some and then, becoming suspicious, alerted the police. From a description and from some remarks Geoffrey had carelessly let slip to the stall-holder, they had had little difficulty in tracking the culprit down.

So Geoffrey was relegated to the status of a shabby sneak-thief and Charles had either to concede that Hugo had killed Charlotte or start investigating somebody else.

The only two people left who seemed to have had any emotional relationship with Charlotte were Clive Steele and Diccon Hudson. Clive was supposed to have been in Melton Mowbray auditing at the time of the murder and no doubt Diccon would have some equally solid alibi. Still, wearily Charles supposed he must try to get interested again and check their movements. But the spark had gone. Any further investigation was going to be just a chore.

Since he was down in Breckton, he might as well start with Clive Steele at the Backstagers. The Back Room opened at six. Just sit a little longer on the common to kill time.

"Evening, sir. A bit dark to be out here, wouldn't you think?"

He looked up to see the outline of the same policeman who had found him inside the Meckens' house the previous week.

"Yes, I suppose it is dark." While he had been wrapped up in his thoughts, it had changed from dusk to blackness.

"You intending to sit there all night?"

"No, I wasn't. I was just going."

The policeman held his ground and watched Charles out of sight along the footpath towards the Backstagers. He obviously thought he was watching a potential rapist or, at the very least, a flasher.

Charles decided that, considering how low his stock stood with the Breckton police, any alternative murder solution he took to them was going to have to be backed up by absolutely incontrovertible evidence.

There was no sign of Clive Steele in the Back Room, nor of anyone else Charles knew until Denis Hobbs came in at about half-past six. He was his usual boisterous self, though there was a slight strain beneath the bonhomie.

He had come in for a quick one on his way home from work. Charles wondered if he needed his regular drink to fortify him to face the redoubtable Mary.

They got talking naturally and Charles bought drinks. Denis had a pint, Charles a large Bell's. After some social chit-chat, Charles said, "So you've got your man."

Denis recoiled. "What do you mean?"

"Your burglar."

The builder's eyes narrowed. "What do you know about it?"

"I know who's been arrested."

Denis Hobbs looked at him steadily for a moment and then downed the remaining half of his beer. "We can't talk here. Come round to my place for a drink."

Inside, the Hobbses' house was, decoratively, exactly what the mock-Tudor exterior with its brash stone lions would lead one to expect. The tone was set before you entered. A china plaque by the doorbell showed a little girl in a crinoline and a boy in a tasselled cap leaning forward to kiss over the legend "Denis and Mary live here."

It must have been Mary's taste. The same eyes which had chosen her torquoise trouser suit and rainbow-colored lamé slippers had certainly picked the jungle wallpaper. And the Raspberry Ripple carpet. And the green leather three-piece suite. And the miniature cluster of swords and axes tastefully set behind a red shield on the wall. And the three-foot-high china pony pulling a barrel. And the wrought iron drinks trolley with the frosted glass top and gold wheels. Denis was content to let her make decisions about such things. After all, she was the artistic one.

It was to the drinks trolley Denis went first. He poured a pink gin for his wife, a Scotch for Charles and got out a can of beer for himself. When he had poured it into his glass, he crushed the can in his huge paw. The metal flattened like tinfoil.

Mary's greeting to Charles was distinctly frosty. She had not forgotten his reservations about her Madame Arkadina.

But Denis cut through the atmosphere by saying, "He knows."

"What?"

"About the burglary."

"Oh." Mary looked downcast, as if rehearsing for a tragedy.

"How did you find out?" asked Denis.

"I spoke to Vee on the phone this morning. She told me."

"Damn. I hope she's not telling everyone."

"Why? What does it matter? Presumably everyone'll know when it comes up in court."

"If it does come up in court. I'm trying to see that it doesn't."

"I wouldn't have thought you stood much chance. I mean, if the police picked him up, they're going to bring charges."

"I don't know. I'm going to ask them not to proceed. I'm going to stand bail for him and try to keep it as quiet as possible."

"But why? I mean, there's no question as to whether he did it or not."

"No, he's admitted it."

"Then why shouldn't he pay the price of his actions?"

"Well, he's. . . ." Denis was having difficulty in framing his thoughts (or his wife's thoughts) into words. "He's a friend."

Mary took over. "It's terribly embarrassing. I mean, he's been in and out of our house so often. This place becomes a sort of Backstagers' annex when the Back Room closes—particularly when we've got a show on. Geoffrey's a very close friend."

"I can see it's embarrassing, but the fact remains that he has stolen your property."

"Yes, but people are so materialistic, Mr. Parrish. What's a bit of jewellery?" Mary sat surrounded by the fruits of middle class affluence as she posed this ingenuous query.

"The thing is," Denis contributed, "we didn't realize the financial state he was in. We could have helped, lent him some money or something, not driven him to this."

"Hardly driven. He did it of his own free will, presumably to get himself out of a spot." Charles was bewildered by their reactions. Instead of being affronted and disgusted by Geoffrey's betrayal of their friendship, they were trying to justify his actions.

Mary gave Charles the patronizing smile of sainthood.

"It may be difficult for you to understand, but we feel an enormous loyalty to Geoffrey. He is a wonderfully talented person and we just didn't understand the terrible time he had been going through. To steal from us was a terrible lapse, which I'm sure he's regretted bitterly, but it's only an expression of the dark side of his impulsive artistic temperament."

Now Charles had heard it all. That old fallacy about artists being answerable to a different code of morality from the rest of society. It was a view he had never subscribed to in the cases of the extremely talented writers and actors of his acquaintance who had tried it on, but for it to be used in the context of a moderately talented amateur was ridiculous.

Denis Hobbs nodded as his wife continued to expound her views. Charles was saddened by the sight of a man so emasculated by marriage. He wanted to get Denis on his own again and find out what the man really thought, not just hear him echoing Mary's opinions.

"You see, Mr. Parrish," she continued, "it's often difficult to explain to people that we don't just believe in materialistic values, that we have an appreciation of art—the theatre, poetry, painting." She gestured vaguely in the direction of a Hawaiian sunset scene luminously painted on black velvet.

"We've been lucky, we've made a lot of money. . . ," Charles thought it was magnanimous of her to include Denis in this statement. She spoke of money as if it were an unfortunate skin condition. He was surprised Denis didn't get up and knock her block off. But her husband's brainwashing had been completed too long ago for him even to notice the slight.

"So what we feel is, Mr. Parrish, that it's our duty—being of limited artistic talent ourselves—" She simpered in expectation of some complimentary remonstrance, but then remembered Charles's expressed view of her acting abilities and moved hurriedly on. ". . . to share some of our good fortune with more artistic people.

That's why we make this room a second Back Room and provide lots of drinks and things . . ." (She couldn't resist quantifying their altruistic generosity.) ". . . so that we can do our bit for the spread of cultural ideas, stimulate lively conversation, discussion of the arts and so forth."

Charles began to understand her cock-eyed reasoning. Mary Hobbs saw herself as the leader of an artistic salon, the Madame de Staël of Breckton. Geoffrey Winter's crime was just the errant behavior of one of the young geniuses she was nurturing. In fact, it was a challenge to her values, an opportunity for her to show how far above material considerations she was.

He wondered to what extent Geoffrey had anticipated this reaction. If he had known that the theft, if it ever came out, rather than ruining him socially, might increase his stock among the Backstagers and build up his mildly roué image as a man above conventional morality, then it was not such a risk as it might have appeared.

"Oh dear." Mary Hobbs gave a tragedienne's sigh. "I wonder if the police will be persuaded to drop the charges against him."

This abstraction seemed to be directed at Denis. "I don't know, dear. I doubt it. But perhaps Willy will be able to get him off lightly. Our solicitor's looking after Geoffrey," he explained for Charles's benefit.

Good God. The man broke into their house and stole their property and there they were leaning over backwards to defend him. "What'll happen, Denis? Will he be up before Breckton magistrates in the morning?"

"Yes. My solicitor's going to ask for bail. We'll be going down to give moral support. We've got to get him free as soon as possible."

Mary agreed. "Otherwise it's going to interfere dreadfully with *Winter's Tale* rehearsals."

Charles kept having to remind himself that these people were real when they came up with remarks like that. "And then straight on as before . . . Geoffrey rehearsing, no mention of the theft, coming back here for drinks after the Back Room closes. . . ."

"And why not? Geoffrey's a friend." Mary's constant repetition of this was like a child's assertion that someone is "my best friend." In children it is always symptomatic of insecurity and only heard from those who have difficulty in making real friends. And in adults too.

Charles found something infintely pathetic about the Hobbs trying to buy friendship with a constant supply of free drinks and afraid to lose a friend even when he abused their trust so disgracefully.

Denis seemed to think Mary's view of Geoffrey needed endorsement. "Oh, he's a very lively bloke, Geoffrey. I don't suppose you've ever seen him in full flood. Life and soul of the party. Always full of ideas for games and what-have-you. What was that thing he started here after the first night of *The Seagull*, love?"

Mary Hobbs giggled with the memory. "Oh yes, it was a great game. One of you goes out of the room and dresses up and then when they come back in, you all have to ask questions to find out who they're meant to be. You know, you can be politicians or show biz people—or members of the Backstagers, if you like." She laughed again, a comfortable "in" laugh. Her Backstagers' identity was a vital support to her life. "Do you remember, I pretended to be Reggie, the secretary?"

Denis guffawed at the recollection.

"Actually he wasn't very pleased, was he, Den?"

"No, can't take a joke, our Reggie."

"Did Geoffrey himself have to go?" asked Charles.

"Oh yes. He was a riot. He did Margaret Thatcher. He found a wig of mine and a smart overcoat and . . . oh, it was hysterical. He'd got the voice just right, hadn't he, Den?"

Denis agreed on cue. "He was great. Oh, it was a great party, that. Charlotte—she looked really lovely that evening—wore this long check sort of smock thing."

"Yes, well, she's dead," snapped Mary with unnecessary brutality. Denis recoiled as if struck. Mary hastened to paper over the rift. "Oh, it was a marvellous night. We had so much fun. Of course, Charlotte spent most of the evening with young Clive Steele."

This seemed to be put in as another rebuff to her husband. His attraction to Charlotte must have been the subject of some marital tiff. She went on. "Such a clever boy, Clive. And so good-looking. You know, I think he had rather fallen for Charlotte. He certainly seems very cut up about her death."

"I suppose he's only just heard," said Charles.

"What do you mean?"

"Well, he was away working all last week in Melton Mowbray, wasn't he?"

"Oh no, apparently that was called off. No, Clive was here all last week."

Nineteen ...

THIS TIME CLIVE Steele was at the Back Room bar
when Charles went in. The young man greeted him
patronizingly and graciously accepted the offer of a drink.
"Don't know why I bothered to turn up this evening. I get
here to find the rehearsal's off."

"Oh."

"Yes, we were meant to be doing all the Florizel/
Perdita scenes tonight. But Vee Winter's cried off.
Apparently not well."

Or too upset over her husband's arrest to face anyone,
Charles reflected. "You're playing Florizel?"

"Yes. Terribly drippy part. But I suppose I really am
too young for Leontes," he conceded as if youth were the
only possible bar to his being given the lead. "Still, it's
parts like Florizel that need real acting. It takes a bit of
talent to make something of that kind of weed, so I
suppose it's quite a challenge."

Charles saw a chance to move the conversation his
way. "So, but for recent events, it would have been

173

another Clive Steele/Charlotte Mecken partnership. Florizel and Perdita."

"Yes." Clive looked shaken, childishly near to tears. "Oh my God, it was terrible. For her to die—Charlotte who had so much to give—for her just to be strangled by that drunken brute."

"Hugo?"

"Of course Hugo. You know why it was...?" Clive leaned across to Charles confidingly. "Hugo was jealous."

"Oh yes. Of whom?"

"Of me."

"You?"

"Yes. It's no secret that Charlotte and I got pretty close over *The Seagull*. There was a very strong mutual attraction. I think Hugo must have realized and killed her in a fit of jealousy."

Charles was almost amused by the young man's arrogant assurance. "Are you saying you were having an affair with Charlotte?"

"Ssh," Clive hissed loudly and waved his hand in a rubbing-out movement. "Don't say a word about it here." His dramatic behavior must have drawn the attention of everyone in the bar. Fortunately, for a moment there was no one there.

"Well, were you?"

"Not exactly. I mean, nothing had actually happened. You know, she had a few scruples and I didn't want to rush things, but it was inevitable the way it would go. Only a matter of time."

This seemed very much at odds with the state of the relationship which Charles had gathered from the conversation he overheard in the car park. He had surmised from that that Clive had misinterpreted Charlotte's natural niceness as a come-on and that she was disillusioning him in no uncertain terms. But Clive seemed to have forgotten that encounter and retained his belief in his irresistible magnetism for her. Maybe, now she was dead, he found that a reassuring fiction to cling to. It flattered his ego and gave him an opportunity to feel tragic.

He was certainly putting on a performance of feeling tragic. "And now she's dead—it's awful. She was so young, so ripe for loving. I think love is for the young and beautiful." This was clearly a category in which he would include himself. "I mean, it was disgusting, the idea of Charlotte being groped by an old man. Someone like Hugo."

Charles didn't rise to the implied insult. He was a great believer in letting people ramble on when they were in spate. It was a much easier method than interrogation and often quite as informative.

"Or Denis Hobbs," Clive continued.

"Denis? Did he grope Charlotte?"

"Well, he was always putting his arm round her, you know, casually, like it didn't mean anything, but I got the feeling he was enjoying handling the goods.

"There was one night I remember—Wednesday before last it was, first night of *The Seagull*—we all went round to the Hobbses' place. I think Denis must have been a bit pissed, but he certainly seemed to be after Charlotte."

"Oh."

"We'd all decided we wanted to play silly games and Denis kept saying we ought to play Postman's Knock (which I should think is about his level), because that meant kissing people—and he made a sort of grab at Charlotte to demonstrate."

"But you didn't play Postman's Knock?" Charles fed gently.

"No, we played a much better game that Geoff Winter knew. Dressing up sort of thing. But Denis didn't give up. I went upstairs with Geoff to sort out some dressing-up clothes and then I came down while he was changing— actually he got himself up as Margaret Thatcher, he was bloody marvellous—anyway, when I got down, there was Denis with his arm round Charlotte. He was pretending it was all casual again and she was sort of joking, but I don't think she really liked it. And I'm damned sure Mary Hobbs didn't like it. She came out into the hall at that moment and you should have seen the look she gave Denis."

"When did you last see Charlotte?"

"After the cast party."

"That was the last time? You didn't talk to her again or anything?"

"Well, actually I did. I rang her on the Monday afternoon."

"The day she died."

"Yes." Clive seemed poised to launch into another self-dramatizing lament, but fortunately didn't. "I was trying to fix to meet her that evening. The fact is, we hadn't parted on the best of terms after the cast party...."

Ah, now the truth, thought Charles.

"Silly thing, really," Clive continued. "She was talking about leaving Hugo for me and I was saying no, it was too soon, we should let things ride for a bit ... you know, the sort of disagreement you get between two people in love."

Charles couldn't believe it. Clive's self-esteem was so great that he actually seemed to have convinced himself that he was talking the truth. Charles was glad that he had heard the real encounter between the two; otherwise he might have found himself taking Clive seriously.

The young man rambled on mournfully. "So I wanted to meet for a drink, you know, to chat, sort it all out. But she said she couldn't, so I got a bit pissed off and went to the flicks with an old girlfriend."

"Did Charlotte say why she couldn't meet you?"

"She said someone was coming round."

"She didn't say who?"

"Some friend from drama school."

Charles took a taxi from Waterloo to Spectrum Studios in Wardour Street. He told the uninterested commissionaire that he wanted to see Diccon Hudson and was directed to the dubbing theatre.

The red light outside was off to indicate that they weren't recording at that moment, so he went on through the double door. It was a large room, walls covered with newish upholstered sound-proofing. At one end was a screen above a television which displayed a film footage count. On a dais at the other end was the dubbing mixer's control panel. On a low chair in front of this Ian Compton lolled.

He looked quizzically as Charles entered. Some explanation of his presence was called for.

Charles hadn't really thought of one and busked. "I was in the area and I thought I'd just drop in to find out about tomorrow's session. Save the phone call."

Ian Compton looked sceptical and Charles realized it did sound pretty daft. But no comment was made. "No, in fact tomorrow's off, Charles. Farrow's not happy with the radio copy and I'm afraid it's all got to be rewritten. Take a few days. I should think we'd be in touch by the end of the week."

"Fine."

"And don't worry, you were booked for the session, so you'll get paid."

"Oh thanks." Charles's instinct was to say, "Don't bother about that," but he bit it back. He must develop more commercial sense.

Ian Compton looked at him with an expression that signified the conversation was over.

"Actually, I wanted to have a word with Diccon too."

A raised eyebrow. "Really?"

"Yes."

"Well, we're just about to start doing a few more loops. Then we'll break in about half an hour when we've got to set up a new machine."

"May I wait?"

Ian Compton shrugged permission.

The film that was being dubbed appeared to be about a young bronzed man fishing for octopus on a Greek island.

Charles need not have worried about Bland work being done behind his back.

Diccon Hudson was working at a table in a box of screens. He wore headphones. The film was cut down into loops of about thirty or forty-five second durations. On each loop a chinagraph pencil line had been scored diagonally, so that it moved across the screen when the film was run. When it reached the right hand side, it was Diccon's cue to speak, adding his voice to the Music and Effects track.

He worked smoothly and quickly. He needed only one run of each loop and timed the words perfectly each time. A master of all forms of voice work.

When they had to break, Ian Compton went out to the control room, where the new machine was being set up. Charles went into the box of screens. Diccon Hudson looked up nervously. "To what do I owe this pleasure? Coming to get some tips on voice technique?"

"No."

"On dubbing? The great con-trick. Wonderful the things you can perpetrate in dubbing. That bloke on the screen, the diver who does all the talking, is Greek. Talks English like a broken-winded turkey. But by the wonders of dubbing, he can speak with my golden cadences. It's magic. He does his talking at one time, I add my voice at another and in the cinema, so far as the audience is concerned, it all happened at the same time." He had taken this flight of fancy as far as it would go and paused anxiously. "But you didn't come here to talk to me about dubbing."

Charles shook his head slowly. "No, I've come to talk about Charlotte Mecken."

Diccon colored at the name. "Oh yes, what about her?"

"When we last met, you said you used to see her from time to time. The odd lunch."

"So?"

"I've come along to ask if you saw her a week ago today. Last Monday."

It was a shock. Diccon gaped for a moment before replying. "No, of course I didn't. Why should I? What are you insinuating?"

"I'm not insinuating anything. I'm just asking you what you were doing last Monday."

"I was out."

"Out where?"

Diccon hesitated. "Out with friends."

"Friends who I could check with?"

"No, I...." He tailed off in confusion.

"Did you speak to Charlotte that day?"

"On the phone, yes. When I got back to my flat after an afternoon session, there was a message on the Ansafone for me to ring her."

"Someone else she spoke to that afternoon was told that she had a friend from drama school coming down in the evening."

"She wanted me to go down and see her, but I couldn't."

"You went out with friends instead."

"Yes. What are you suggesting—that I strangled her?"

Charles shrugged. "Well, I don't think Hugo did."

"I didn't. I swear I didn't go down there. I went out."

"But you won't tell me where."

Diccon hesitated and seemed on the verge of saying something. But then, "No."

"But you did speak to her?"

"I've told you, yes. She wanted my advice."

"On what?"

"She wanted to know if I knew the name of an abortionist."

This time it was Charles who was put off his stroke for a moment. "But she wasn't pregnant. The police post mortem showed that."

"Well, she thought she was. And she said she'd decided she couldn't keep the baby."

"Why not?"

"I don't know. Presumably because Hugo didn't want children."

"You think it was Hugo's?"

"Why not?"

"Not yours?"

"What?" His surprise seemed genuine. "Good God, no, I never scored with Charlotte, I'm afraid. Though I tried a few times."

"Then why did she ask you about the abortionist?"

"I don't know. I suppose I was the only person she knew who might have that sort of information. I have been around with quite a few women, you know," he added with a touch of self-assertive bravado.

It had the ring of truth. If Charlotte had wanted to get rid of a baby, in her naïveté, she wouldn't have known where to begin. She could only ask a friend. Why not Sally Radford? Perhaps Charlotte knew of the girl's emotional reaction to her own abortion and didn't want to upset her by asking.

As to the pregnancy, that must have been a phantom, some freak of Charlotte's cycle, probably a side-effect of going on the Pill.

But if what Diccon had said was true, why was he being so evasive about the night of the murder? "I'd like to believe you, Diccon, but I'd feel happier with an alibi I could check. Where were you at the time Charlotte was strangled?"

"I . . . I won't tell you."

"You tell him." A new voice came into the room, harsh and electronic. It was Ian Compton on the talkback from the control room. He must have had Diccon's microphone up and been listening to their conversation for some time.

Diccon turned towards his friend behind the glass screen and shouted, "No!"

"All right then, I'll tell him."

"*NO!*" Diccon Hudson rose and ran out of the screens towards the glass as if he could somehow smother Ian's speech.

But the talkback talked on inexorably. "Diccon was

with me. We went together to a club called The Cottage, which you may know is a resort of homosexuals or gays as we prefer to call them. We went there because we are both gay."

"No," muttered Diccon, tears pouring down his face.

"For some reason, Charles, as you see, Diccon does not like to admit this fact in public. God knows why. He's only discovered his real nature recently and still tries to put up a straight front. That's why he lunches all these pretty little actresses, like Charlotte Mecken—to maintain the image of the great stud. Which is in fact far from the truth."

Diccon Hudson found his voice again. "Shut up," he said feebly.

Charles decided it was time for him to go. He didn't want to get into a marital squabble and he didn't think much more useful information was likely to be forthcoming. "I'm sorry to have caused a scene. Thank you for telling me all you have. It's going to help me clear Hugo."

"Clear Hugo?" Diccon repeated in amazement. "You can't still think that I—"

"No, not you."

But something that Diccon had said had released a block in Charles's mind and he was now certain who had killed Charlotte and how.

The next day he was going to confront that person.

Twenty...

CHARLES FELT CERTAIN that the person he wanted to see would be at Breckton Magistrates' Court the next morning.

It was nearly twelve o'clock when the little group came out of the main entrance. Geoffrey was in the middle with Vee, and they were flanked by Denis and Mary Hobbs. A man in a pin-striped suit, presumably the Hobbses' solicitor, followed slightly behind. The atmosphere was more celebration of the return of a conquering hero than the release on bail of a man accused of petty theft from a friend.

Charles went forward to meet them. "I'm terribly sorry, Geoff. Vee inadvertently told me what had happened."

"That's all right. Thanks for coming." Geoffrey wore a mask of relaxed affability. "I suppose everyone will know soon."

"Yes, but it'll blow over pretty quickly," asserted Denis Hobbs. "Don't you reckon, Willy?"

"We live in hope," the solicitor replied smugly. Charles wondered whether smugness was something that all solicitors have to take on when they're articled in a sort of primitive ceremony like a circumcision rite.

"Anyway, don't let's talk about it," said Denis. "Charles, we're all going out to lunch—how'd you like to join us? We're going to put all this behind us and think of the future. I hadn't realized how badly things were going with poor Geoff. But I think over lunch we might have a bit of a discussion about one or two openings there might be for architects in my business."

He looked to Mary for approval. She smiled and he glowed visibly. So that was it. Not only was Geoffrey going to be forgiven for his crime; he was also going to get a new job to sort out his financial problems. Mary Hobbs loved being in the Lady Bountiful position, using her husband's money and influence to share a little of the reflection of Geoffrey's talent. And to gain power over him.

Charles declined the lunch invitation with thanks, but said he'd walk along with them a little way.

He fell into step beside his quarry. "I wonder if we could have a chat at some point. Something I'd like to discuss."

"Certainly. How about this afternoon? I'll be at home when we get back from this lunch."

"Okay, fine."

"About three."

Charles nodded It had all been very casual, but they both knew it was a confrontation.

The house was empty but for the two of them.

"Well, Charles, what can I do for you?"

No point in beating around the bush with social pleasantries. It had to be direct. "I know how you did it."

"Did what?"

"Killed Charlotte."

"Ah." Charles had to admire the other's control. Even

total innocence should have given more reaction. "So that's what it is, is it? All right, intrigue me, tell me how I did it."

"It was a very carefully worked out plan. A work of genius, one might say."

"I'm touched by the compliment, but I think it may be misapplied. Incidentally, before you tell me how I committed this crime, would you be so good as to tell me why I did it?"

"You did it, Geoffrey, because Charlotte told you she was pregnant and as a good Catholic she said she wouldn't have an abortion. So you had to get rid of her out of loyalty to Vee. She was coming to see Vee the day after she died. She'd fixed it by phone. You couldn't risk Vee finding out about the pregnancy. It would have destroyed your marriage."

Geoffrey left a pause before he responded. Maybe it was in reaction to what he had heard, but when he came back, his voice was as firm as ever. "I see. So that's why I did it. Now perhaps you will continue with telling me how I did it."

"Right. Last Monday night, after we parted at the main road, you went home. Vee wanted to watch *I, Claudius*, as you knew she would. As soon as it had started, you put on a previously prepared cassette of yourself doing the lines for *The Winter's Tale*, then left this room by the balcony. You walked briskly along the path at the back, over the main road and—"

"Look, I hate to break in on this magnificent piece of deduction, but I would just like to congratulate you and say you're absolutely right. Except in one detail. I did all this, but the crime which I committed in the time thus gained was not Charlotte's murder, but the theft from Denis and Mary for which I appeared in court this morning."

"If you will wait a moment, Geoffrey, I was coming to that. This is where your plan was so clever, because it involved a double alibi. If anyone worked out the cassette dodge, then you had a second line of defence that during the relevant time you were doing the robbery. On Friday you thought I was on to the cassette—in fact, you flattered me, I hadn't quite got there by then—but that was sufficient to frighten you into implementing your second plan, getting rid of the stolen jewellery in such an amateur manner that you knew it was only a matter of time before the police arrested you."

"I see." Geoffrey's voice was heavy with irony. "So, according to the Charles Paris theory, in the time I had at my disposal, I stole the jewellery and strangled Charlotte in two different houses half a mile apart. Hmm. You obviously have a very high opinion of the speed at which I work."

"No, I haven't finished the Charles Paris theory. What I am saying is that you didn't do the robbery."

"Oh, I see. Magic, was it? The jewellery suddenly appeared in my pocket. Or maybe I had a leprechaun as a henchman and he spirited the stuff away. Was that it?"

"No. You did the robbery, but you didn't do it on the Monday evening."

"But that's when it was done. That's when Bob Chubb saw the light in the Hobbses' house, that's when the police came and found it had been done."

Charles shook his head slowly. "All you did on the Monday night was to break the window, open the catch and leave the switched-on torch on the window sill, so that Bob Chubb or whoever else happened to pass couldn't fail to see it. You'd actually taken the valuables on the previous Wednesday evening when you'd been round at the house. You'd put a lot of planning into the thing. You'd suggested the game of charades at the Hobbses' and while you were upstairs dressing up as Margaret Thatcher in Mary Hobbses' clothes, you helped yourself to the jewellery.

"So, on the Monday, you only had to stop at their house for thirty seconds rather than five minutes. That was why everyone was so surprised at the tidiness of the burglary. Everything left as if it hadn't been touched. It hadn't been. No one went inside the house that evening.

"The crime was done like a dubbed film—one part of the action at one time and the other later on. The theft was committed before the break-in. And everyone thought they had been done at the same time."

Geoffrey's face remained impassive. Impossible to judge what was going on behind that mask.

Charles pressed on. "Then you went to the Meckens's house. It was easy. Hugo played into your hands. Apart from the convenience of his constant outspoken attacks on Charlotte, you knew he wasn't going to leave the Back Room until it closed. And that then he'd be in a state where his reactions and memory could play him false.

"Charlotte was all set up. You'd seen her at lunchtime. In the excess of your passion you'd marked her neck with a lovebite, so you knew she'd have a scarf round her neck. Maybe you'd even said you'd drop in, so that she'd open the door quickly and you wouldn't be seen.

"Strangling her must have been quick. She was totally unsuspicious, off her guard. Then you put her body in the coal shed to delay its discovery and you were off home. Back before the end of *I, Claudius*. Just in time to pick up from the cassette and start bellowing your lines with such vigor that your next-door neighbor was bound to complain, thus even getting the police to corroborate your first alibi."

There was a long pause. Geoffrey kept the usual tight rein on his emotions. "Well, Charles, you give me credit for a lot of ingenuity."

"I do."

"And I can see that, if all your assumptions are correct, it would have been possible for me to kill Charlotte. But you need a ripe imagination to follow the twists of what you've just told me. I think you might have difficulty persuading the police of it all—particularly as at the moment they have two crimes and for each one they have a self-confessed criminal."

"But Hugo only confessed because he couldn't remember and because he didn't care."

"If he didn't care, then why should we?"

"I don't know. I just want the truth to come out."

"Admirable sentiments. Well, I'm sure as soon as you can produce evidence to back up your preposterous allegations, the truth will come out."

Yes, there was the rub. Charles knew he had nothing except his own convictions to support his theory. It was right, but, as Geoffrey observed, it was going to be almost impossible to persuade the police to take it seriously. Particularly if the persuader was someone who stood as low in the estimation of Breckton Police Station as Charles Paris.

He felt his confidence begin to ebb and, with an effort, tried to regain momentum. Maybe he could shock a confession out of Geoffrey. "What makes the whole crime so ironic, even tragic, is the fact that Charlotte wasn't even pregnant."

"What!" This time Geoffrey reacted. This time, for a moment, the mask crumbled. And from that instant Charles knew for certain that he was right. He might have got some of the details of the plan's execution wrong, but Geoffrey Winter definitely killed Charlotte Mecken.

"No," he continued coolly. "The police post mortem revealed that she wasn't pregnant."

"But—"

"Oh, she thought she was, but it was just some freak effect of her going on the Pill. If she'd had the nerve to go to her doctor about it, he could have quickly disillusioned her. But no, she told you she was pregnant; she said, as a Catholic, she was going to keep the baby and, what was more, if you wouldn't tell your wife about it, then she would. When she made that decision, she signed her death warrant."

Geoffrey's eyes were closed and he was breathing deeply. Charles turned the knife in the wound. "And, if you're looking for further ironies, between the time that she saw you on the Monday lunchtime and the time that you killed her, Charlotte had decided that she would have an abortion. She rang up a friend for advice on how to end the pregnancy that never was. So her death was doubly unnecessary."

Geoffrey was badly shaken, but he rallied. There was only slight tension in his voice when at last he spoke. "This has been very interesting. May I ask what you are going to do now, Charles?"

"Nothing. I'm going to go away. I'm going to leave you with the knowledge that I know exactly what happened and see how you react. Maybe you'll come round to the conclusion that you ought to devise another equally ingenious method of disposing of me. My knowledge makes me just as much of a threat to your way of life as Charlotte was."

"You sound almost as if you are issuing a challenge."

"Yes, Geoffrey. I am."

Twenty-One...

THE NEXT FEW days were an agony of vigilance for Charles. He hadn't really meant to challenge Geoffrey to kill him, but without evidence he saw no other way of drawing the man out into the open. All he had to do was to keep on his guard and see Geoffrey before Geoffrey saw him.

In case the worst happened, he wrote down a detailed reconstruction of what had taken place on the night of Charlotte's murder and lodged it with Gerald. Then if Charles Paris were found murdered, it could be delivered to the police, who would know where to start looking for their murderer.

But Charles didn't intend to be murdered; he intended to catch Geoffrey Winter attempting to murder him. That attempt would be tantamount to a confession to Charlotte's murder.

Charles tried to live as normally as possible. He stayed round Hereford Road a lot, so that Geoffrey should have no difficulty finding him. He drank less, so as to remain alert. He rigged up an elaborate alarm over the door of his bedsitter so that he should not be surprised in the night. And he waited.

Meanwhile he tried to continue his career, as funds were getting low. In this he encountered an unexpected setback.

He rang through to Mills Brown Mazzini on the Friday to find out when the next Bland recording session would be. Ian Compton told him with ill-disguised glee that the housewives of the Tyne-Tees area had given the thumbs-down to the Mr. Bland television commercials. They had found the animation too frivolous for something as important as a bedtime drink and they didn't like the name.

As a result, Ian had worked out a completely different approach for the product, and it had been approved by Mr. Farrow. The new campaign for the drink (now renamed Velvet-Sleep) was to feature a young couple who had just finished a hard day's decorating. The voice-over was going to be done by Diccon Hudson.

So that was it. Charles was paid off for the Tuesday's cancelled recording session and suddenly the heady vistas of infinitely repeated commercials bringing in infinite repeat fees shrank down to a few solitary session payments. Needless to say, there had been no long-term contract signed. The dazzling prospects had existed only in conversations between Charles and Hugo. With his sponsor still remanded in custody, Charles was suddenly out of the voice-over world. He never heard the result of the No Fuzz test.

He ran Maurice Skellern and said he would audition for the Cardiff company. He had to live on something.

He also kept thinking he should ring Frances, but didn't get round to it.

On the Saturday morning he received a letter.

• • •

Dear Mr. Parrish,

Thank you so much for letting us see your play, *How's Your Father?*, which we read with some amusement.

We regret that we do not feel it to be suitable for our World Premières Festival, as we feel it is too slight and commercial a piece for production in what has increasingly become one of the main outlets for modern experimental theatre in this country.

We have also been fortunate to receive a new play by George Walsh. It is called *Amniotic Amnesia* and concerns the thoughts of a group of foetuses awaiting a fertility drug-induced multiple birth. It raises many interesting questions of philosophy and ecology and is much more the sort of work we feel the Backstagers should be doing.

We will hope to see you down here for our next production, *The Winter's Tale* by William Shakespeare.

> Yours sincerely,
> Robert Chubb
> World Premières Festival Sub-Committee

PS Your script is being returned under separate cover.

It was over a week before the truth sank in. That Geoffrey was not going to be drawn, that so long as he didn't rise to Charles's challenge, he was safe. He knew that there was no evidence and he did not intend to supply any.

Charles felt ridiculous when this dawned on him. He had nothing; he should have realized. Geoffrey Winter had killed Charlotte Mecken, but it could never be proved.

Charles was furious. Having got so near, to be thwarted at the end... Hugo would be sentenced to life imprisonment and maybe come out after eight years to drink himself to death. Geoffrey would get a fine or a short sentence or maybe—if Willy, the Hobbses' solicitor, were really good—a suspended sentence for the crime he'd had to commit as a cover-up. Then he'd take up a job with Denis Hobbs in the "construction industry" and continue to play all the leads at the Breckton Backstagers. And Mary Hobbs would have the satisfaction of feeling that she had done something direct and positive for the artistic life of the community. And memories would heal over and the case would trickle away.

He couldn't stand the thought. He resolved to get back to Breckton for one last try. There must be something he had missed.

It was Monday. Exactly two weeks from the night that Charlotte had died. Monday, November 15th. It had been a bright autumn day, but was dark by the time Charles arrived once again at Breckton Station.

Nearly seven o'clock. Instinctively he walked towards the Winters' house. As he rounded the corner of their road, he stopped.

Geoffrey and Vee were walking ahead of him towards the main road.

Of course. Rehearsal. Up to the Back Room for a quick one, and then ready to give artistically at seven-thirty. Leontes and Perdita, played by Geoffrey Winter and Vee le Carpentier. The stars of the Breckton Backstagers. Oh yes, he knocks around a bit with other women, but they're really very close. No children, no. But they're very close.

He tailed them at about fifty yards distance, but they didn't look round. It was uncannily silent. Geoffrey, like Charles, must be wearing his favorite desert boots and Vee's shoes also must have had soft soles, for there was no sound of footfalls on the pavement of the footpath. Just the occasional chuckle from up ahead. Geoffrey sounded more relaxed alone with his wife than Charles had ever heard him in company. Oh yes, he needed Vee. When Charlotte threatened that relationship, she had to go.

Charles followed them all the way, keeping the same distance behind. It was sickening. He knew what had happened, the criminal was right in front of him and yet he could do nothing about it. Nothing without proof.

By the time Charles got to the Hobbses' house, Geoffrey and Vee had disappeared inside the Backstagers. Everything went on just the same—drink, rehearsal, home, work, drink, rehearsal.... Why should he try to break it up? Hugo was long past hope—what did it matter whether he despaired in prison or at large? He had nothing to live for. Geoffrey Winter at least had his love for his wife, his acting, his little affairs. What was the point of trying to break that pattern?

Charles decided he would go back to the station, get the train back up to Town and forget the case had ever happened.

A feeling almost of nostalgia for the time he had spent retracing Geoffrey's movements made him take the long way round past the Meckens' house?

It stood dark and unfriendly. Presumably, after Hugo's trial it would go on the market, someone would buy it. There would be stories of what had happened there. If the buyer were imaginative, Charlotte's ghost might even be seen. If not, it would all be forgotten. Sooner or later, all would be forgotten.

As he stood there, he was seized by an impulse to do it once again. One more retracing and that was it.

This time just as Geoffrey must have done it two weeks before. He slipped across the gravel drive to the side gate. He no longer cared about the net curtain snoopers. Let them report him if they wanted to. He was about to leave Breckton for the last time.

The side gate was not locked. He lifted the latch and let himself into the back garden. He had a small pencil torch in his pocket and he shone it on the ground before his feet as he walked towards the coal shed.

It was a shock not to find Charlotte's body still there. That embarrassingly sprawled figure had so etched itself on his subconscious that he felt cheated when there was only coal in his torch-beam.

He stood there for a moment looking round. Nothing. Not the perfect crime, but a crime that was by now undetectable. Maybe at the time, maybe if Geoffrey had been the first suspect, there might have been something which would have given him away. Maybe the blood from the abrasion on Charlotte's neck had been on his hands as he walked home. But if so, that blood had been long washed away, long dispersed and unidentifiable. Now there was nothing. Not a chance of anything.

Charles's footsteps crunched in the coal-dust as he sighed and left the coal shed. Back across the drive, along the road and down the tarmac footpath to the common.

There was no one about, of course. No one to see him, just as there had been no one to see Geoffrey Winter a fortnight before.

He walked doggedly along the hard mud path skirting the football fields towards the path to the main road. He passed the untidy bit, the dumping ground, still dominated by the washed-out crater of the Guy Fawkes bonfire.

He reached the paved path and walked a couple of paces. Then he stopped.

He felt a little tremor of excitement. Twisting one foot round on the paving, he heard the crunch of coal-dust.

Good God, it stayed on. He'd have thought it would have been wiped off by the walk across the common, but no. The little grains of coal embedded themselves into the rubber sole of the desert boot and took a lot of shifting.

And if he had noticed the difference in sound when he came on to the paving, so would someone else have done two weeks before. Could Geoffrey have taken the risk of carrying that incriminating dust into his own house?

No, surely he would have tried to remove the evidence. Charles looked at his own sole with the pencil torch. Little chips of coal glinted in the beam. He tried to scrape them off. Some came, some stayed. He could have got them all out, but it would have taken time. And time was the one commodity which Geoffrey hadn't had. His tape gave him a maximum of forty-five minutes.

And on the morning Charles had visited him in his office, Geoffrey had been wearing new shoes.

Charles looked round. There was only one obvious place to dispose of a pair of shoes. You could throw them into the bushes, but there they'd be retrieved by the first nosey dog who came along. But in the bonfire....

After all, so long as suspicions were held off for four days, the evidence would be burnt publicly and no one any the wiser. And as soon as Geoffrey heard about Hugo's arrest, he could relax. He had only to wait till November 5th to be absolutely secure.

But sour Reggie had reckoned the fire was out of control and it had been doused by the fire brigade. There was still that soggy mess of ash. If Geoffrey had shoved the shoes into the middle at the bottom to be inconspicuous, there was a long chance that they might still be there.

Charles scrabbled through the damp debris of ash, half-burnt sticks and charred rubbish by the light of his torch. He spread it all flat on the ground. There was nothing big enough to be a shoe. One half of a heel might have come from a lady's sandal, but otherwise nothing.

He sat down deflated, mindless of the debris. Oh well, it had been a good idea. Too easy though, really. Geoffrey wasn't stupid. He'd have found a way round the shoes, scrapped them or changed them, destroyed them at home. Or just put them high enough in the bonfire to ensure that they would burn quickly.

No, the case was over. Charles put one hand down on the ground to lever himself up.

And felt close round a soft flesh-like lump.

He had the object up in his torch-beam. At first it seemed to be a plastic-covered ball, which had survived by rolling to the bottom of the fire before it was doused. It was shapeless and blackened with ash.

But then he saw that it had once been a pair of plastic gloves, rolled together. Now deformed and fused by the heat, but recognizably a pair of gloves.

But that wasn't what brought a catch of excitement to his throat. It was the fact that the gloves had been wrapped round something. Something soft.

The melted plastic had made a little envelope which gave easily to his fingernail. Inside, preserved like a packet on a supermarket shelf, was a handkerchief.

A blue and white handkerchief he had last seen when Geoffrey Winter had lent it to him in the Back Room. On the night of Charlotte's murder.

The brown smudge across it showed why it had been thrown away to be burned in the fire.

It was blood.

Blood that could be identified by a police laboratory.

Blood from the scratch on Charlotte Mecken's neck.

And was it fanciful for Charles to catch a hint of a familiar expensive scent?

As expected, the police took a lot of convincing. When he first started to expound his reconstruction of events, Charles could feel how unlikely it sounded.

But when he showed them the handkerchief, they got more interested. After about an hour they agreed to go up to the common with him to look at the bonfire. A plain-clothes man and a uniformed constable.

They didn't talk much. They inspected the scene and started assessing times and distances. Charles didn't push his luck by saying anything.

Eventually the plain-clothes man spoke. "Well, it's just possible. Of course, we won't really know until we get this handkerchief looked at by forensic. But I think we'll go and talk to Mr. Winter, get his version of events. Where did you say he lived?"

"He won't be there at the moment. He's rehearsing a show for the Breckton Backstagers."

The rehearsal was in full swing when they arrived. The cast were doing the awakening of the statue of Hermione.

The queen stood frozen center stage, with Geoffrey as Leontes on one side of her and Mary Hobbs as Paulina on the other. Vee, as Perdita, knelt behind her husband. By her side stood Clive Steele as Florizel.

As Charles and the policemen entered at the back of the rehearsal room, Geoffrey was declaiming. They stood in silence while he continued.

> "O! thus she stood,
> Even with such life of majesty,—warm life,
> As now it coldly stands,—when first I woo'd her.
> I am asham'd: does the stone rebuke me
> For being more stone than it? Oh—"

As he acted, Geoffrey took them in. Charles could see the pale grey eyes flicker from him to the uniformed policeman, then to the plain-clothes man and finally come to rest on the soiled handkerchief which the detective was still holding gingerly in front of him.

When Geoffrey saw the handkerchief, his voice wavered. There was a little gasp like the beginning of a giggle.

The supposed statue of Hermione let out the snort of a suppressed laugh. Then Mary Hobbs went off into uncontrollable giggles. Vee and Clive started laughing too.

None of them knew what the joke was, but soon all the Backstagers in the room were roaring their heads off. It was one of those moments that often happen at rehearsal, when suddenly a tense scene breaks down into the ridiculous. A mass "corpse."

Gradually, one by one, the actors stopped, slowing down to gasping breaths, and wiping tears from their eyes. Then they turned to look, with growing concern, at Geoffrey Winter.

But he just kept on laughing.

YOU'LL BE MAD FOR THESE MYSTERIES BY

Simon BRETT

Set in the sophisticated world of British theater, they star amateur sleuth, Charles Paris.

_____ AN AMATEUR CORPSE	10185-9-23	$3.50
_____ A COMEDIAN DIES	11371-7-17	3.50
_____ CAST IN ORDER OF DISAPPEARANCE	11123-4-59	3.50
_____ MURDER IN THE TITLE	16016-2-17	2.95
_____ MURDER UNPROMPTED	16145-2-11	2.95
_____ NOT DEAD, ONLY RESTING	16442-7-11	3.50
_____ SITUATION TRAGEDY	18792-3-21	2.50
_____ SO MUCH BLOOD	18069-4-19	3.50
_____ STAR TRAP	18300-6-26	3.50

_____ **YES,** please enter my order and also send me future information on other Dell Mystery paperbacks.

_____ **NO,** I'm not ordering now but am interested in future information on other Dell Mystery paperbacks.

At your local bookstore or use this handy coupon for ordering:

**DELL READERS SERVICE—DEPT. B1056A
P.O. BOX 1000, PINE BROOK, N.J. 07058**

Please send me the above title(s). I am enclosing $_____ (please add 75¢ per copy to cover postage and handling). Send check or money order—no cash or CODs. Please allow 3-4 weeks for shipment.
CANADIAN ORDERS: please submit in U.S. dollars.

Ms./Mrs./Mr._____

Address._____

City/State._____ Zip._____

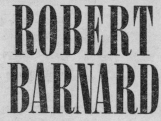